The
SUPERMARINER

Part 1

-Mathew George-

Copyright © Mathew George, 2012

All rights reserved. No part of this publication may be reproduced, stored in a retrieval system or transmitted in any form or by any means electronic, mechanical, photocopying, recording or otherwise, without the prior written permission of the copyright owner.

Cover photograph: Consolidated Commodore, Miami. Courtesy of the State Archives of Florida

Acknowledgments

The sources I consulted during the writing of this novel are too numerous to mention but my abiding interest in the subject began when I attended a lecture as a War Studies undergraduate at King's College, London. It was given by a former WAAF who had been based at Pembroke Dock during the War. Her tales and anecdotes, with all their accompanying 'hwyl', left the entire room enraptured and have stayed with me ever since.

Author's Foreword

I have never had much time for fiction. The abiding wisdom of history has always taken precedence over any imaginative flight of fancy. So I resolved, as soon as I had abandoned my peripatetic ways, to chronicle a unique era when the term 'aviatrix' became prevalent. I didn't consider my inability to fly to be an impediment, until I was given flying lessons whilst working for a courier company in Thailand. Only then did I experience the emotive fervour that flying induces, which only rhetoric can sufficiently convey.

But a passion for flying can not entirely explain the motives of the pioneering British women who took the glamour of flying to heights not witnessed before or since. Determined, and often ingenious, eccentricity is part of a wider tradition that has shaped our history – an analysis of which would go beyond any biographical remit. I have therefore been unable to write a cold, clinical history but I have made every effort to retain the same accuracy that a historian demands. All of the main protagonists are fictitious but the historical context is entirely real.

M.G.

For Piglet

1

University had little to offer when confronted by such loss and despair. I languished in its corridors like steerage, listening to the choristers bleeding and the fruitless filibustering on the stairs. Every day was a Sunday afternoon filled with books forever promising and every time I scaled the library, its galleries let out a square-pegged groan.

All my passions had been taken from me and now they lay abandoned, miles away. The newspaper clippings I had accrued meant nothing to anyone and the hours of tinkering in my workshop at home had all been a complete waste of time. My silly, boyish enthusiasm for all things mechanical began to slip away, until it was suddenly arrested by a bus shelter chanting 'Join the Auxiliary Air Force today!'.

I didn't need much encouragement: I knew there was an RAF airfield fairly close by because my studies would often be interrupted by the distant gurgle of an aero-engine. Every time I heard it I would shut up my books with a thud which rendered the librarian pale. When the newsreels began to speak of another war as providence, I finally abandoned my scarf in my room. I cycled out of town sniffing for the twinkled haze of castor oil and exhaust fumes.

A barrier saluted me at the entrance as if angling for new blood. I was directed to the Duty Officer and I made my pitch in front of his desk, paraphrasing chunks from the recruitment posters. He jotted down my particulars with a reckoning gaze, before leaning slowly towards me.

"So, you want to learn how to fly, hey?" He finally asked.

"Yes, sir, that's correct," I replied.

"Have you done any flying before?"

"No, I'm afraid not, sir."

"Do you know anything about aircraft?"

"Well, I've been interested in flying for many years. I've been to the Hendon Air Display and - "

"Yes, yes but do you actually know anything about flying?" he interrupted.

"Oh, well, yes. I think I have a good grasp of the basic rudiments. I don't have any hands-on experience, that's mostly confined to tractors and steam cultivators," I said, with a slight smile. "But I've always tried to keep abreast of developments."

My girdled voice echoed away as the sepia-stained windows exhibited the airfield in stills. He laid his notes to rest in an empty wire tray before slowly stiffening.

"I see." he said with hard-boiled eyes. "Well, I must explain to you that this isn't a civilian flying club. I get a lot of young chaps coming in here during their lunch hour, hoping to either become the next Richthofan or else they simply want to take their girlfriends up for a spin every now and again. We're not looking for heroes and we're not after Champagne Charlies. The object of the exercise is to find recruits for the Auxiliary Air Force so that, in the event of hostilities, we can fill in any gaps. Do you understand?"

"Yes, sir."

"Above all" he continued, "we're looking for competent flyers, who are prepared to maintain their standards with regular practice twelve months a year. Is that clear?"

"Yes, sir."

A fitful low then interrupted his rumblings and he strained to see over the sill behind him. His chair let out a sinewy sigh as a pair of stocky biplanes descended onto the grass. They bounded along in tandem until corralled by ground staff outside a wooden pavilion.

"I tell you what." he said, standing up and marshalling me out the door. "I'll see if I can find one of the instructors. They might be able to give you a better idea as to what we're after. It's a fairly quiet day today, so just wait here a moment."

He headed off toward a crop of stout parley that had gathered around the two machines. The crowd disappeared inside the pavilion and the sound of beer and condiment serenaded the aircraft, as they sat puffing on funnels inserted in their fuel tanks. They bore little resemblance to the sleek monoplanes I had seen at air displays; but they exuded menace with their serpent-like insignia and poisonous yellow wing flashes. I was about to creep over and take a closer look when a group of puckered choristers dribbled out from the pavilion and began wading across the grass. They reared up to time, knee-deep in buxom lyrics until they disappeared through a break in the hedge; another figure then emerged at the doorway dressed in purged white overalls. He simply nodded sharply and set off toward me with a freshly-dusted swagger.

"Hello there young man," he called out, knocking back his sticky hair with his fingers. "Sorry to have kept you waiting. So you're another of our new recruits, are you?" he said, shaking my hand. "Come on over to the Clubhouse, it's a bit quieter in there now. We can have a chat and you can tell me a little about yourself."

With a smile that seemed to be pulled by strings, he led me inside the hallowed retreat for pioneers; I perched upon an easy chair, amid press-ganged furniture that leaned-to, ready to barricade the windows and doors. Pranks and feats scampered along the walls, beatified in black and white and I waited expectantly, ready to hear of the sacrifices pinned to the beams, instead of lifting them laboriously from a page.

It wasn't long, however, before the same questionnaire began again and my expectant gaze was tossed aside by a reticent authority. I tried to brighten our acquaintance with titbits of what I knew; but I was consigned to the fringes of another lazy afternoon. He simply sat quietly sizing me up with his starched outfit creaking like cold chiffon; all my advances were shushed by a hissing gramophone that sat abandoned at the far end, on top of what looked like an altar table.

"Well, I've got to shoot off early today," he said standing up smartly, "but I tell you what, we can continue with this session at the same time next week."

The long-awaited meeting of minds ended with a dull clank and I baulked at his surrendering smile and another harmless handshake.

"I can show you around the base, as well. You can meet some of the staff." he added after a pause. "That should give you a better idea about what this RAF lark is all about."

I remained still, seemingly stung by scruple. But, perhaps, unwittingly my gaze heckled his stance. As he prepared to break out another polished stoop, he gently loosened one hand from his pocket, as if he were about to offer me some cigarettes or stockings.

"I tell you what," he said, "if there's a machine available, I'll take you up for a spin as well. How does that grab you?"

"That would be – fine," I replied cautiously; hoping, at last, that there might be something to grasp at, amongst so much courtly stricture and indifference.

2

The filleted remarks which I'd had to endure at my induction were gradually forgotten; even the looming gantry of finals became obscured by the thought of my first flight. When I strolled across the airfield the following week, all I could see was a lawn cut by low-flying propellers and the ribbons in full bloom across my instructor's chest.

There was no preliminary chatter. We began with a series of tests to evaluate my eyesight and reflexes; these were followed by another question-and-answer ding-dong. When I had finally convinced him I wasn't too dim-witted, he then began guiding me through the basics of flying, using a blackboard he'd set up outside one of the huts.

From behind a nervous grin of teeth, he slowly illuminated the depths of the cockpit with a devotion which bore sentences in duplicate and triplicate. The sermon progressed with the seat of the pants being eschewed by concerns that seamed across his face, like tyre marks on the road. I sat bodiced and bonneted as I listened to his instructions and began nodding my head with increasing rapidity. But, after an hour or so, he finally laid his finger down and glanced up at the heavens, before computing a response.

"Come on let's get upstairs before that front gets any closer." he said, ushering me into one of the huts. "We can probably squeeze in a couple of circuits and you can see what I've been talking about."

He hauled down a thick flying suit from its peg and then presented me with a musky, leather helmet, garnished with cotton wool.

"Right. All set?" he asked, straining at the door as I was still fumbling with the buttons.

Without waiting, he marched toward a bright yellow biplane parked outside the hangar, which he introduced as a De Havilland Moth. He stepped around the machine, keeping me at arm's length and repeated all the words he'd uttered outside the hut. But, with the helmet flaps tightly buckled, I heard next to nothing - just the thump of a gavel from inside the hangar, as my dull collegiate routine was sent down.

"OK, that's enough chat. I'll take her up and go through a few manoeuvres. But don't touch any of the controls," he warned, "just enjoy the ride."

He strapped me into the front seat and the down-belows eye-balled my constitution, while the aircraft was being checked, primed, pumped and cranked. With a dumpling gaze, I watched smoke and flame snake out from the exhaust stack and the blast from the airscrew smacked into my face. The plane was hustled forwards and the clamour of 'what'll she do, mister?' was quickly drowned out.

Tobogganing over the bumps, the fuselage rocked back sharply, springing up off its heels and the wings began see-sawing on the currents. A body that was only as drunk as it wanted to be, held me in its tortuous grip, paying out my entrails as we bowled along like a hoop. The plane tore up my daft illusions and, panting in despair, I slid further down into my seat. I sat with my head bowed while the instrument panel swayed its fingers and the joystick staggered about between my knees.

Eventually, I dared myself to peer out over the side and, as I did so, all my laments suddenly counted for nothing. I looked down upon a tobacco tin and tea-caddy backdrop, where cars were grazing in carborundum and cows were clocking off. Poo-pooing hamlets stood shivering in their terraces while piebald fields lay tanning in the sun. Figures pointed up as we ransacked the landscape with dirty fumes and hellish clatter, while the heavens looked on, puffing on a shag of nonchalance. A machine stuck together with glue made from fish bones had, somehow, delivered a near-collapse of reason; it was saved only by a blanching jolt and the sound of wheels rubbing along the grass of the airfield.

Perhaps, we had been in the air for just a few minutes. But, as the plane trickled to a halt, I peeled off my flying helmet and sat bent in a monkish stupor, with my tongue beached on the floor of my mouth.

"And I never want to see you flying like that." A voice cackled from over my shoulder.

I looked round to see my instructor lit up by a full-bloodied smile; all the plimsolled neatness had been spoiled by a Mickey Mouse silhouette and a sprinkling of grass.

"So what did you think? Did you enjoy it?" he asked, helping me up out of the cockpit.

"Oh yes. It was good fun. A little hairy at times."

"Oh you'll get used to it," he champed, "it's only your first time up. In fact, I was very easy with you on that trip. I could have done some rolls and a couple of loops but I wasn't sure if you'd had any lunch."

He slapped me on the arm approvingly and we ambled back to the Clubhouse, where he reverted to the same favoured chair.

"I think we both deserve a drink after that, don't you?" he said, pulling a hip-flask out from underneath the cushion. "So you think you've got what it takes for this flying lark?"

"I hope so." I replied. "It's certainly a lot more exciting than anything University has to offer."

"Good show," he said tipping back his flask. "What is it you're studying, again?"

"Classics," I replied, hoping he wouldn't be too disappointed.

"Oh yes. That's right. And how long have you got left to run?"

"Well, my finals are coming up this summer."

"And any plans for after university?"

"No, not really."

"Well, I'm sure something'll turn up. Although the job situation isn't too good for anyone at the moment."

"Actually," I said, gazing outside at the Moth. "I was

hoping that learning to fly might open a few doors."

"Don't count on it. There's hardly anything available career-wise, especially for someone without any experience; it's the old story of too many pilots and not enough planes," he said, offering me some brandy as consolation. "They're only looking for part-timers, at the moment. Trust the bloody politicians - doing things on the cheap as usual."

"Would a knowledge of engineering be of any use?" I asked, prodding him a little further.

"Maybe. A good pilot should always know his big end from his O-ring," he said squeezing out a flimsy grin. "But one thing's for sure - a degree in the classics certainly isn't going to be much help. I suppose what we really need is another war," he concluded, glancing down at a newspaper in front of him. "That would do wonders for everyone's career prospects."

"Did you fly during the War?" I asked, peering once again at his ribbons.

"Not quite, no," he said hesitantly, while his fingers drummed the side of his flask. "I was in the Navy back then. I spent most of my war on board a destroyer in the North Sea. Just my luck - as soon as I transferred to the Royal Naval Air Service, all the action was finished."

"So, how did you come to be in the RAF, may I ask?"

"I didn't have a lot of choice. After the War there were nothing but cutbacks and in-fighting. I stuck it out in the RNAS for as long as I could. But, after the RAF took over, nobody seemed to want us Navy pilots and I got sick of risking my neck in wartime relics or hand-me-downs from the Air Force. Even after all these years though," he said looking down at his tunic. "I still haven't quite got used to the colour of this uniform. Not quite the right shade of blue, is it?"

We both chuckled politely as his well-worn patter petered out, before a debrief of the flight began. Now, however, the lofty bearing was gone and he held me in his grasp, baiting his wisdom with anecdotes about aces on the Western Front.

"That must have been a proper show. Ever since then we've had nothing to do except bomb unruly tribesmen in various parts of the Empire. And there's not much fun in that I can tell you. I've never felt less like a gentleman in all my life," he sighed, looking out the window.

"Come on," he then said standing up abruptly and trailing his scarf toward the door, "we've still got time for one more flight, if you're up for it?"

I hardly needed any encouragement and we both stepped outside to bask in the Moth's painted rays. Without waiting for any of the ground staff, he swung the propeller and immediately gave me my first taste of the controls. He jogged alongside the aircraft, guiding me forwards, while I taxied her toward the end of the airstrip.

As soon as we were airborne, he dangled me by the ankles and began buzzing the airfield in tight figures of eight. The aircraft strumpeted across the sky until the light began to fail and, finally, he brought the Moth back down to Earth. We finished the lesson sitting together on the running board of a petrol bowser; there he spoke almost as if he were alone. He began telling me of some of the other Royal Navy fliers, who seemed to have been scattered like chaff on the wind.

"One of the shorter chaps, 'Winkle' we used to call him, tried his hand at being a jockey. He seemed to think that flying would be just like riding a horse. He didn't get very far," he laughed, "although I did watch him race in the Grand National once."

"Have you never been tempted to rejoin the Navy?" I asked.

"No, not really," he replied briskly, as if scratching out his mind's eye. "Nothing's changed - and I don't suppose they'd welcome a deserter back with open arms."

3

I could now barely tolerate the sight of bent bodies wasting themselves on ink fumes. They seemed to stagger beneath the volumes in the library, as they pulled at them like lintels. The only way to dispel the lethargy was with another visit to the aerodrome. But this was increasingly offset by the failure of my allowance to appear in my pigeonhole.

Nevertheless, I continued my flying lessons and my enthusiasm for the Air Force blossomed amid the elements. Each week, I cycled along the blind lanes trying to glimpse the grubby ground staff and the shanty of lonely huts. The same brace of *Avros* were always there to greet me, sitting like furniture with their varnished veneers and cobwebbed rigging.

But one afternoon my gaze was stolen by a twin-engined monoplane which I'd not seen before. It sat poised on the airstrip, posturing with a grace I'd thought only nature could afford: the fuselage seemed to have been hewn in a single stroke, before being dipped in red preserve.

An edifice of blue tunics were gathered around it, booming out in stately voice; marooned among them was my instructor, who glanced toward me grasping his cap, as the ignition rendered them all breathless.

"Superb, isn't she?" he called out, cantering up to my side.

"Yes, terrific. What is it?" I shouted back.

"She's called the Comet - de Havilland's new long-distance air racer. She's just broken the London to Cape Town record. That's what all the celebration is about."

I looked around to see the crowd brimming with pride and we all waved to the pilot one last time. The delicate thoroughbred trotted to the end of the 'strip where the engines idled breathlessly for a few moments, before releasing a glorious howl. The aircraft galloped towards us but, as it sped by, something seemed to be binding tight amid its pistoned strains. I yelled out to my instructor, who was still beaming excitedly and we both watched as the machine began porpoising, like a fat man trying to get over a wall. It bounded into the long grass, before ripping through a wire fence. Both sides of the undercarriage were torn off and the fuselage skidded across the turf, before, finally, burying itself in the hedgerow.

We all surged forward at a sprint to find the plane lying on its belly with a broken wing, sighing a cloud of dust and debris. The pilot had been torn out of his seat harness and now he was either dead or unconscious. As they pulled his face away from the shattered instrument panel, an ambulance motored up furiously ringing its little bell. It swallowed him up and then sped away, leaving the crash site like a crippled circus act.

Nothing was left except an amalgam of sciences spread-eagled in the bushes. The fuselage wept scuffed paintwork and the engine blocks cooled with a death-watch tick. In no time at all, however, the rudder-and-stick jockeys around me were picking like seagulls:

"What a shambles," one of them glibly remarked.

"It's lucky he was only carrying enough juice to get to Croydon. The whole thing would have probably gone up like Vesuvius if he'd been on full tanks."

They pencilled in a copper-bottomed mortality which I'd scorned as just a footnote and my labrador instincts begged me to wee, wee, wee all the way home.

"I'm afraid there won't be any flying lessons today," my instructor grumbled with his hands in his pockets. "But why don't you come along at the same time tomorrow? They'll have all this mess cleared up by then and we can go for another spin."

As I stood ovulating a response, I couldn't help but look up at the once amicable ether, which so many great minds had failed to master.

"Hey, come on, don't look so worried," he went on, taking me to one side, "it looks a lot worse than it is, you know. This old girl'll be flying about again in a couple of days, you can be sure of it. In fact, I tell you what," he added with a wistful glint. "it's about time you had a proper crack at the controls. No more bunny-hopping around the airfield. A real cross-country jaunt this time. How does that grab you?"

"Is that an order?" I replied.

"Yes," he said, cranking up his smile. "Prangs like this are par for the course. The best remedy is to jump straight back into a kite and forget all about it. Now come on, let's go and wash all this down."

He pulled me toward the pavilion, brewing up more fighting talk. But when we reached the doorway, he turned back to watch as the wreckage was slowly being cajoled across the mud.

"They'll find out what the problem is soon enough. But what was it you yelled to me just as he was starting his run? I didn't quite catch it."

"Oh, it was nothing really. I just thought something sounded a bit - tappety. That's all."

"Well, everything sounded OK to me. And if he wasn't getting full boost, he would have aborted."

But I wasn't so sure. 'Good show' was more than just an casual remark in the Air Force. It was the benchmark - and anything less than that, it seemed, was punted into the long grass and quickly forgotten.

4

That night, I took refuge in a winceyette world as I watched the Comet being smashed upon the bleached walls of my room. Suddenly university had become a worthy monument to monotony and each time I left its cosy confines, all I could see was machinery bristling with sharpened extrusions.

When I returned to the airfield the following afternoon, I was sure I was being watched by gremlins with cross-haired vision. Instead of heading straight toward the Clubhouse, I took a few moments to check over the Moth; I gave all the struts a good yank and was just about to lift the engine cowling, when my instructor strolled out through the door.

"Oh come on, you've got nothing to worry about. She's been thoroughly checked over. You'll have the time of your life. Just forget about yesterday," he said, laying a large road map out over the wing. "This is the plan for today. We're going to head to a small aerodrome about 150 miles west of here. It's a route we call the Steeple Chase - 'cos all you have to do is follow this line of churches," he added, pointing to a procession of crucifixes on the map. "It's quite straightforward. What I'll do is take her up to a safe height and then, when I want you to take the reins, I'll tap you on the shoulder. Alright? And, if you need me, I'll be right behind you," he assured me with a wink.

We both climbed aboard the Moth but, as the prop was about to be swung, a staff sergeant jogged up to the side of the plane.

"There's lightening reported about 5 miles from here, sir, heading our way," he informed my instructor. "I wouldn't advise going up."

"I'm not frightened of a bit of water, Sergeant. You should know that," came the response.

Both voices were singed by the engine's frosty exhaust and the plane strained on its stitches. We took off in a ticklish flurry and I quickly ran through all the golden rules laid down the week before; I was desperate to adopt the same effortless artistry my instructor always displayed. But, as we passed the first church steeple, he tapped me on the arm and I found myself jousting in a swell beneath a simmering grey porridge.

I reached out and throttled the joystick, while my feet clutched the rudder pedals. An eager breeze connived with the torque of the motor, while a distilled contempt swirled about inside the fuel tank. Even basic manoeuvres were a struggle and, for much the time, it seemed as though I was simply shadow-boxing the plane's movements. The aircraft wormed between my fingers, continually spoiling the alchemy of airspeed and angle of attack.

I clung on as best I could but soon a fierce cross-wind was ballooning the linen sides of the fuselage. It threatened to whip us into a spin and its fury began to hatch like lice upon my goggles. The trickle quickly became a downpour, leaving me almost blind; but I grimaced through the rain, making increasingly futile adjustments until a hand, once again, touched my arm.

The Moth shrugged off my grasp and we turned back toward the aerodrome. I looked round, expecting to see my instructor cowering like me behind the aero-screen. But he was sitting completely at odds with all the other components, which seemed to be trembling almost uncontrollably. With an emphatic thumbs up, he descended through the squall until the airfield reappeared; we touched down, splashing through puddles that left the top wing dripping like a chandelier.

"Come on, hurry up. I'm getting wet," he called out as I struggled to extricate myself from the swollen wicker seat.

"How did I do?" I called out, flapping after him in my sodden overalls.

"Fine. Fine. You managed to keep her pretty much straight and level, which is pretty tricky on a day like today. So well done. I thought we'd better head home as it's a bit too wet to be flying about in an open cockpit. But we can have another go next week."

We waded back to the Clubhouse where a group of young pilot officers were gathered by the notice board just inside the door.

"Come on. Make way you chaps. I'm getting wet," my instructor barked.

They shrank with a collective 'sir' to the far end of the room, where they slumped like puppets onto the chairs and settees. I began moulting my wet flying gear, while my instructor stood gazing imperiously at the announcements on the board.

"Ah, I'd forgotten about that," he said, unpinning a piece of foolscap. "It's the annual Brats' Bash in a few weeks to mark Trenchard's birthday. You still haven't been introduced you to any of the other Auxiliary chaps. Would you like to go along?"

"I'd love to. I'll have finished my exams by then," I blurted out, before a sticking point came to mind. "But how much are the tickets? My funds are getting a little tight."

"I don't think they're very expensive. If you like I'll see if I can wangle you an invitation."

"Oh, I don't want to put you to any trouble, sir."

"It's no trouble. Got a slight cash flow problem at the moment, have you?"

"Yes you could say that," I confessed, as we sat down. "In fact, at the moment, it's looking rather terminal."

"How's that come about all of a sudden?"

"I'm not sure exactly," I said, hesitantly. "You see, I usually get a small allowance. But, since my father passed away, I haven't received anything for a number of weeks. I can only assume there's been some sort of - complication."

My insignificant noises were then overpowered by a sharp declaration at the other end of the room. One of the pilot officers turned away from pressing his nose against the window and he pleaded up to the rafters.

"Damn it all!" he yelled. "The one day we need to do some aerobatics and look at it. None of us are going to make the team for Hendon if we can't put on a decent show at Manston this weekend."

"Well – we could rehearse our manoeuvres in here?" one of the other officers sniggered, as he struggled to light his pipe. "It'll be good practice for my ball-room dancing."

"Oh, don't be such a clot."

"No, wait a minute. That's not such a bad idea," added another posy-faced canvas.

"What on Earth are you going on about?"

"We've each got a car, haven't we?"

"Yes. But what use is that?"

"Well we could run through our set-pieces," he said, standing up. "At least we'd sort out how we're going to formate on one another."

"That's the most stupid blinkin' idea I've ever heard."

"Anything's better than sitting in here all day." Another officer retorted. "Why don't we give it a go."

"Alright," most of them agreed in chorus.

"But my roof leaks like hell."

"Here, I'll lend you my cap. Catch."

They paraded past us and, as they opened the door, a gust of wind evicted a copy of the *Daily Sketch* from beneath my instructor's chair.

"Oh, I was going to show you this," he said, picking it up and removing a page. "There you go. You were quite right about that Comet yesterday. It was a problem with the valve gear," he said, lifting an eyebrow almost in salute. "But what I'd like to know is - how does a Classics undergraduate manage to figure that out before anyone else?"

He leaned forward, as if ready to make notes and I grappled for a moment with my usual reticence: the knowledge I had gained from within my little workshop was considered, at best, unnecessary and, at worst, eccentric - especially at house parties or croquet.

"Well I come from a farming background," I replied after an unsightly pause.

"That doesn't really answer my question," he persisted with a bemused grin.

"Well, there was always machinery to be repaired and the job of maintaining it all often fell to me. I've always enjoyed tinkering."

"Somehow, I didn't have you down as a farm boy," he said, looking increasingly puzzled. "Fair size, is it, this farm of yours?"

"There was always something to keep me busy."

"And what do you keep - livestock?"

"That was up to the tenants on the estate. But there were fishing rights and pheasants to look after. We also held horse trials and one day eventers and, of course, it was always extremely busy during the hunt season."

"By Jove, this isn't some small-holding, is it?" he exclaimed, as if peeping through the railings. "Sounds like a bloody great pile. Why on earth are you messing around with Greek and Latin - or even learning to fly, for that matter, if you have this estate or whatever it is, to look after?"

"Well, I have a couple of older brothers," I stated, as the horse hairs in the seat began digging into my behind. "That probably also explains why my funds have suddenly dried up."

"Do you not get on with them?"

"Well, let's just say they probably won't have any use for me, now that my father's gone."

"Doesn't sound a very wise strategy, laying off the chief engineer."

"I doubt they've given it a second thought."

"Are they not interested in horticulture and the like?"

"No, not at all. They've both got a full-time job looking after their creditors."

"Oh I see. That's the problem is it?" my instructor said gravely. "Daft system really. Offspring just don't seem to pop out in the right order, do they?" he concluded, looking up at a portrait of the King on the wall.

Perhaps it was the ease with which he swallowed the story, but the thorny shadow in my voice didn't precipitate the same sense of disgust or despair. For once, I was ready to go on and tell him about my brother's still-born motor-racing career - and the spare parts I had machined for him to within one sixteenth of an inch. But, ironically, we were interrupted by car engines revving outside.

"What the hell are that lot up to now?" my instructor muttered, getting up.

I joined him at the window where we both watched half a dozen cars careering about on the grass. There was a brief attempt, of sorts, to choreograph a flying display but it quickly degenerated into a race around the huts.

"Bloody hooligans. Never thought I'd see the airfield getting beaten up by some bloody motor cars," he grumbled, as mud splashed the windows. "If that lot had ever landed on a carrier they wouldn't be frightened of a bit of wind and rain, I can tell you. Too many fair-weather pilots in the RAF that's the problem. It's all about close formations and display flying and all that sort of nonsense. I'll bet none of those chaps out there has ever even fired a machine gun. Let alone hit anything." he scorned as the foggy panes shook, marking another lap. "Are you a good shot? You should have had plenty of practice," he said, returning to his seat.

"Give me a gun and I wouldn't go hungry."

He grinned smartly and began warming his hands on knees.

"Well I tell you what, as soon as you've done your first solo we can fly down to Sutton Bridge and do a bit of target practice. That's always good fun," he said, before lowering his voice. "Don't let on about it just yet, though, the brass are usually a bit stuffy about that sort of thing. That was another good thing about the Navy. You could do live firing whenever you liked; no need to worry about upsetting anyone or breaking any windows. Having said that," he continued with a glint, "when we were at Scapa Flow we used to go and shoot up this old disused lighthouse. But on one occasion a couple of the boys got lost in cloud and they hit the wrong one. Took quite a few drinks with the lighthouse keeper to sort that little mess out, I can tell you," he laughed raucously, before picking up the announcement he had plucked from the notice board. "But I'll say this much for the RAF they know how to throw a good party. The Brat's Bash is usually a good laugh. As I say, I'll see if I can get you a ticket."

"Will you not be going yourself?" I asked.

"No, no. That sort of thing isn't for pensioners like me. But I'm sure you'll have fun."

But all I could envisage was a baptism of belly-laughs where the monikers were handed out free-of-charge. I would probably leave early, having been given a name like 'Cocky' or 'Caesar'. Or, worse still, I'd be completely ignored.

5

There had always been a gentle motion to college life; it had involved little more than catching and throwing back lectures and tutorials. But once I had taken my finals, I had to tug on my savings like knotted sheets toward the conclusion of my flying lessons.

Every week I journeyed to the aerodrome wanting for nothing, except my fix from the candy-floss emulsion. But every week I watched my little yellow biplane emerge from a tarpaulined world which seemed to be disappearing from beneath my fingernails. There was little I could do to support myself in a town already burgeoning with menial academics. Meals became less frequent and I was reduced to drifting aimlessly among the abandoned bicycles.

When my funds finally expired, a large, brown envelope appeared under my door, like a doormat with UNWELCOME inked on its barbed bristles. I processed to the aerodrome for the final time, almost deranged by my own bad breath. Everything seemed to exist in its own Utopia: tram conductors rattled past in their people limousines while daffodils and patisseries sat meditating in shop windows. I sneered at every contented gaze as I contemplated my own future - labelling brown specimen jars in a museum basement.

It was only fitting that when I reached the Clubhouse an unfamiliar voice seemed to bar my entrance. I peered in at an open window and saw a middle-aged civilian slumped in a chair opposite my instructor. His face was creased by concern and he puffed profusely from a pipe that almost airbrushed his suit into the discoloured seat fabric.

"Well I am sorry to hear about Victor," my instructor said slowly, leaning gently toward him. "He was a nice chap, your brother. I read about one of your 'boats having a prang in the newspaper. But it didn't say very much - certainly didn't mention any casualties."

"No everyone got out pretty much in one piece. But poor old Vic was clouted on the head – probably by the fire extinguisher of all things. Complications developed and the little hospital in Ceylon couldn't do anything to save him."

"So what happened exactly? Was it some sort of mechanical failure?"

"No, he either hit an obstacle in the water or simply misjudged his approach."

"Oh, but Vic was too good a pilot to make a mistake like that."

"Well, you know what it's like landing on water. You just need it to be a bit too choppy - or even a bit too calm and it's quite easy to make a real hash of things; we're forever repairing damaged hulls and airframes. In fact, after Vic died I really was tempted to chuck out all the seats and go back to being a mail carrier. At least canvas bags don't mind getting wet."

"Are you still flying those Commodores you picked up

cheap."

"Yes, unfortunately and they're getting pretty long in the tooth now. But of course, we're in no position to replace them. We're having to cannibalise spare parts just to keep what we've got flying. Quite frankly, it's got to the point where I really wonder if there's any future for passenger aviation - simply because of the economics involved. You remember all the fuss there was about airships and dirigibles; everyone said they were the future. Now of course even the Huns have turned their back on all that. And I can't help but feel that maybe airliners are going to go the same way."

"I have to say that running an airline always struck me as a rich man's game," my instructor said, pointing toward a periodical lying on the table in front of them. "The only people I ever hear travelling by air are these fancy film stars."

"Well none of them fly with us unfortunately. It's mostly faded gentry and civil servants. But if someone like, say, Leslie Howard flew with us just once, we'd probably get enough publicity in these society columns to last us for the rest of the year."

"There just aren't enough film stars to go around are there?" my instructor laughed. "Maybe you should move to the other side of the pond, there's far more of them over there."

"Believe it or not that's not such a bad idea. The Yanks are always opening up new routes. Flying seems to be a more acceptable way to travel over there. And, of course, in places like the Caribbean they have the weather on their side. It's not like that for us."

"Well, Stan, I wish I could help. But I'm all tied up here. Besides I'm not sure if I'd be much use; I'm a bit out of practice with all that sort of thing."

"You'd pick it up again pretty quick. And its Navy pilots who are best qualified to handle a flying-boat."

"What about the rest of the old gang? Have you tried asking any of them?"

"Yes - they're all otherwise engaged, unfortunately. But listen don't worry, I'm sure we'll survive. My youngest has started helping me out."

"Oh, how are the girls these days?" My instructor enquired. "Still the same headstrong pair?"

"Yes, though I don't get to see Kitty very much these days. She's settled down with this doctor in Kenya now. I only wish her sister would take a leaf out of her book."

"She's still treading the boards, is she?"

"No, not anymore she decided to pack it in. Can't say I'm disappointed. I was never very happy about her gallivanting around London on her own. And with Margaret gone it's nice to have someone around the house. My biggest mistake, though, was teaching her to fly. Now she fancies herself as one of these 'aviatrix'. She's been taken in by all this nonsense she reads in the 'papers."

"Just your luck to have a couple of daughters," my instructor mused.

"Yes, just my luck," the civilian said reluctantly as he rose up out of his chair. "Well, I'd better be off; if I had more time I'd challenge you to a game of billiards," he added, pointing toward a new addition occupying the centre of the room.

"That thing only a appeared a couple of days ago. No idea where it came from," my instructor said as they both shuffled toward the door. "Darn sight easier to play on than that table they had on *HMS Eagle*. Do you remember, it was rigged up on a giant gimbal?"

"Of course I remember. I always thought it played pretty well in anything less than a Force 9 - won a few bob off you, as well."

"Maybe that's why I didn't like it," my instructor chuckled.

They stepped outside together while I hid behind the cover of a damp textbook, which I was supposed to have studied for a written test. I leaned up against the corner of the Clubhouse but neither of them noticed me; they both watched as a biplane came into land in a series of boisterous bumps.

"Good God. I hope that's not one of your students," the civilian remarked.

"No, no. I'm not sure who that is. We've just started re-equipping with Gloster Gladiators; someone's obviously decided to take one up for a test drive."

"Needs a bit more practice by the looks of it. Haven't you got your hands on any monoplanes yet? That thing looks just like the kites we used to fly together."

"Yes, bloody museum pieces really," my instructor shrugged. "But they were probably cheap to buy. You know the story."

"Good to see I'm not missing much," the civilian said, squeezing my instructor's arm. "Well, it's been good to see you again, old chum. Enjoy the Port."

"Yes thanks very much for that, Stan. I don't know why you thought you had to bring me a present. Besides good stuff like that needs to be enjoyed with at least half a dozen fine paintings - and you've got far more of those than me."

"I don't have quite as many as I used to," the civilian sighed, as his trousers began chattering around his ankles. "Right, I'd better be off, otherwise Madam will give me the sack."

He slowly adjusted his hat and then set off at a plod across the grass. My instructor watched as if checking the line and depth of his furrow, before turning around.

"Oh hello. You're early," he said, looking toward me. "Good to see you studying the Bible."

But for once I couldn't reciprocate his easy smile; I felt like a fraud and the intimate surroundings of the Clubhouse set upon me as we walked inside. I bit down on every image before it was taken away for good and simply shunted through the motions: carelessly discarding the textbook, I changed into my overalls and drudged toward the plane without saying a word. The ground crew seemed to appear from the hanger like minders, eyeing me with suspicion as I ran my bored hands along the tail. As soon as the engine was fired up, I rumbled her down the 'strip, jerking the joystick until we were airborne. Within the midst of the propellered whirlwind, I fumbled through the pleats of our cocktail days together, while the breeze caressed my face. I threw the plane into each manoeuvre, burning the fuel as fast as I could. I churned up the turf on landing before jumping down from the cockpit. I had given a performance that deserved the slipper and I simply hoped my instructor would storm off in disgust.

"Well, I didn't think much of that," he said, ripping off his helmet and goggles. "What the hell's got into you? Are you feeling alright?"

"Not really," I muttered, as he leaned across to tackle my gaze. "I'm sorry, sir, but this'll have to be my last lesson. I've run out of money and I can't find any work."

"Oh, I see. That little problem still hasn't sorted itself out then?"

"No - and I've got to vacate my room in a week."

"That's a shame. You were coming on very nicely and you're pretty close to getting your wings," he said, leaning against the fuselage. "But I can sort out a transfer to another airfield, if that helps."

"No, no, there's nowhere near where I live – unless you have a car. And I think my motoring days are behind me – for the time being at least."

I spelled it out on a cake and expected him to snuff

things out with the usual aphorisms. But instead he stared down from his lofty pedestal, until one of the ground staff finally approached the plane.

"Is everything alright, sir?" he enquired cautiously.

"Yes, yes, fine," my instructor said brushing him aside, before turning back toward me. "Listen, I can't promise anything but leave this with me, would you? I might be able to sort something out. Oh and here, I almost forgot about this," he said, handing me an envelope. "Here's your ticket to the Brat's Bash this Friday. Go and let your hair down. You look as if you could do with some cheering up."

He held it out in front of me but I simply stood smothering my hands in my pockets.

"Go on, you can have it on account," he said, thrusting the ticket into my overalls. "And I'll see you there myself - if I've got any news. As I say, I can't promise anything. But don't leave town just yet."

6

I mostly confined myself to my room over the next couple of days, while I waited for the Brat's Bash. I tried not to dwell upon what my instructor had said; but even the most banal influences toyed with my hopes. Somewhere down the corridor, the morbid strum of a cello set all my memories of the RAF subsiding like a wedding cake. I lay back upon my bed in resignation, until the joyous glow of the light bulb left me blinded by roundels.

I dug out my best suit which I hadn't worn since my father's funeral; but I felt sure it was suitable attire for what was bound to be a hymnal occasion. When I arrived at the aerodrome, I found a large crowd already besieging the Clubhouse: spangled officers and silvered men were swaggering about like foghorns crossing the equator. Jokes were being delivered on the end of a sword and laughter was erupting in salvos.

An eager breeze led me into the fray with my chin up like a periscope. I began looking around for my instructor amongst officers who were busy discussing death in statute - or aeronautics as if it were some black art. I drifted around all the medals on display but couldn't see him anywhere; and whenever I dared to ask, uniforms simply closed around me like curtains.

I persevered until my faith began to desert me and all I

could see were the canapés scattered about on the grass. It was no longer the same hallowed place and a life stuck between high-speed sewers and slow-running telegraphs seemed to beckon. I was just about ready to leave but stopped for a moment, near the billiard table that had once enjoyed pride of place inside the Clubhouse. There was a small crowd watching a game between two well-oiled officers. Standing among them was what looked like another student pilot, who was inexplicably holding a pint glass in each hand. His situation only became clear as I stood next to him, finishing my drink.

"Here Victor, I've found you a batman!" a red-eyed lieutenant suddenly bellowed. "Everyone should have one of these."

He put his arm around me and the other student, who had already been commandeered.

"Oh good show!" another terracotta warrior responded, lurching toward me. "Here. Hang on to that my good man. The waiters around here are like policeman. Never around when you need one."

He handed me his pint glass and leaned across the table, as if he were struggling to get into bed. Holding the cue like a rifle, he then took a shot which went ludicrously wide.

"Damn and blazes!" he yelled.

He immediately had another shot - but this time he aimed at the dickie-bowed flotilla slowly orbiting with the hors d'oeuvres.

"For God's sake you miserable lot, I'm starving," he

said, poking one of the waiters with his cue. "How much longer before you serve something more than just mouse food. At the rate you lot are going, this'll be the only game of billiards where bad light stopped play."

There was a hoot of laughter and the other student pilot chuckled nervously, as if there was a quota to be reconciled. He then looked across and his pale features began flitting around me like a spotlight.

"I think I've seen you on the college square, haven't I?" he enquired at last. "I didn't realise you were part of the Auxiliaries as well."

His face did seem vaguely familiar but, with his crushed collar and ghastly knitted tie, he looked more like a First Year. Nevertheless, I smiled at him through seared lips and we kept up a scripted dignity.

"My name's Brazier, by the way. Although everyone here calls me Smalls," he said, before lowering his voice. "Got off fairly lightly, I suppose."

The crowd then let out a cheer when it was finally announced that dinner was served. We scrummed into the Clubhouse where the officers reclaimed their beers. They shuffled along banqueting tables, which stretched across the room like wings. Myself and Brazier were ushered to a small table by the window, where we were joined by two more student pilots. They were both somewhat older and simply greeted us with a polite growl. The four of us then sat forlornly facing one another, like survivors in a lifeboat, while the food was rationed out by silver service.

We fumbled with the condiments in mitten-like hands before nibbling like squirrels. Around us, men bit down on their cutlery and flashed frightened girlfriends like gold fillings in the midst of their conversations.

"So is your instructor somewhere here?" Brazier finally asked, puffing some small-talk into the air.

"No, I can't see him anywhere," I shrugged.

"What's he like? Do you get on with him?"

"I haven't any complaints."

"I must say, I think I've been a little unlucky with my instructor – he frightens the life out of me. Every time I go up with him I feel sick. I've lost count of the number of near-misses we've had with trees and pylons. That's him over there."

He pointed toward an officer in a rococo dinner jacket, whose cheery glow was suddenly undone when he caught our gaze. He raised his glass in our direction but a large laceration across his face brought on a hideous contortion instead of a smile.

"The trouble is he's only got one eye," his frayed pupil went on. "Apparently he lost the other one during Bloody April. Mind you - the one he's got left seems to be on the blink most of the time. If you pardon the pun."

Brazier's one-eyed instructor then got up from his seat and began dancing past the waiters like a matador.

"Hello chaps," he called out. "Enjoying yourselves, I

hope."

He drew up a chair at the head of the table and began swinging his head around to get a better look at us all.

"I've seen you before," he said looming in on me with his one good eye, while the other remained harmlessly aloof. "Canary is your instructor isn't he? So is he teaching you to fly or to swim?" He laughed like jolt from a pot hole, before drawing in the rest of the table. "Oh I do love a good excuse to dress up. That's what I love about the RAF - best club in the world. There's none of that parade-ground nonsense they insist on in the Army. And remember my boys, the British Empire stands on our shoulders now not theirs. We are the thin blue line, the Imperial police force." He puffed like a mighty oak. "When I was stationed in Somaliland we put an end to years of tribal unrest in just a couple of weeks. All we had to do was drop a few bombs and that was that. We showed the fuzzies alright. We had more trouble from the tsetse fly," he laughed.

He then stood up and proposed a toast to the 'Mad Mullah and his Dervishes'.

"A not-so worthy adversary," he concluded to a roar of applause.

He finally called time on his sermon with us and danced back to his seat clutching his glass like a balloon.

"Goodness me, I don't think it's the fuzzies we need to worry about, these days," Brazier uttered, rolling his eyes.

"Probably not," I conceded quietly.

"To be quite honest," he said confiding in me. "I only joined up 'cos my faculty insisted. They said it would be good practical experience. I'm an engineer, you see. I'm starting an apprenticeship with Rolls-Royce next month. But I have to say, I can learn just as much from models – the RAF planes are so old-fashioned. If the Germans kick off again, I don't fancy getting involved. Not with the kit they're flying."

His remarks made me feel a little uncomfortable and didn't go unnoticed on the other side of the table.

"You know in the last war," one of the older students suddenly erupted, "you would have been shot for cowardice for making a remark like that."

"I'm sorry, I didn't mean to cause any offence," Brazier insisted.

"Well you're doing a pretty good job of it," he snapped like a terrier. "First, you make disparaging remarks about a senior officer who is also, I might add, a war hero. On top of that, you're now saying that, if there is another war, you've no intention of fighting."

"No, I never said that," Brazier protested, raising his voice. "I never said I wasn't prepared to fight."

"Then what are you saying exactly?

"What I am saying is that the Royal Air Force is ill-prepared to fight."

"And what makes you so sure?"

"Because I have been to Germany and I have a brother who fought the fascists in Spain."

"And that makes you an expert does it?"

"Well I can tell you with absolute authority that the Nazis are not fighting with biplanes, like we've got. They have machines that can do over 300 miles per hour. Machines armed with cannons. Machines that will run rings around our Gladiators and Gauntlets."

Brazier's voice then cracked and his eyes began to well. But instead of capitulating timidly, he rose up from his seat and glanced around at all the other tables.

"What I am saying, sir, is that the RAF is not a modern air force. I have seen it for myself - and my brother saw it for himself just before he was killed. What's more, I'll give this warning – that our nation is fated unless we can achieve parity with the likes of Herr Daimler and Herr Benz. The same goes for the rest of the free world. It won't matter how gallant you or I or all these other officers may be. It will be Bloody April all over again."

The room was now silent and all the decorations went a little dull. The scrambled eggs and dignitaries sat muted like coolies; there was no stampede of protest as Brazier sat down, without seeking any sort of apology.

"You have to stay ahead. You can not tame modernity and progress," he murmured quietly, nudging his cutlery into line.

What he had said was clearly blasphemy for some, but nothing got past a grumble. Conversations slowly started up again but, strangely, it was the waiters who seemed to take umbrage. To a man, they stopped serving our table and when dessert failed to appear, Brazier got up once again. He cleared away our plates and returned with three trifles.

"I think I'd better be off. I don't want to ruin everyone's evening," he said, draped in a frail voice.

As far as I was concerned, the evening had never got out of the blocks; and it didn't seem right that Brazier's lonely exit should accompanied by nothing more than hooded brows chewing like sheep. I caught up with him at the door and, together, we walked back through the night. As if by mutual agreement, we steered around the more thoughtful topics of conversation. Instead we both quickly immersed ourselves in the latest exploits of Eyston, Campbell and Cobb. But when we finally reached the gates of our college I stopped him just as he was about to wander off to his room.

"So, what about Mr Rolls and Mr Royce?" I asked. "Are they really just sitting on their hands?"

"Well," Brazier smiled, "not if I've got anything to do with it."

7

I had become used to waking a little short of breath, ready to spend another day awash with concerns. But the morning after Brazier's stark proclamation, I felt almost relieved. The Air Force had little to offer except, at best, a painless end in some quaint anachronism. I should have seen it myself, every time the hangar doors were pushed open. All the aircraft, even the front-line fighters, were just a negligee of matchstick struts and doped membranes. I had watched the riggers repairing the airframes using the same techniques I had learnt as a boy. Perhaps, in some way, I had found that rather comforting, knowing I could have lent a hand - if only I'd had my penknife and a hefty length of elastic.

Now, at least, there was no need to extend my credit any further and I began packing my things away. There were no more false hopes; I was heading back to a house standing with its shoulder to the door - and a future where everything would be prefixed by 'just'. I had had my fill of boyish thrills, all paid for by His Majesty's government. Now I was glad to be getting out before things got too serious.

As I was filling up my trunk, however, there was a knock on the door.

"I'm sorry to bother you, sir, but this telegram arrived just a moment ago," the porter announced with a satisfied gaze. "by motorcycle despatch rider."

When I saw the Air Force insignia stamped on the envelope, I shut the door on him like a cuckoo. I sat down on the bed and a clinical typeface barked out a request that I return to the aerodrome that evening. It might as well have been signed by 'Hobson' or 'Murphy' because I had sold my bicycle earlier that afternoon. I ended up having to hail a taxi back to the aerodrome which cost me almost as much. Of course, I didn't want to go; but as I waited alone among the locked hangars, I reasoned that, at least, it was a chance for me to say a proper goodbye to my instructor. I sniffed around the drab olive sundries growing on the airfield until eventually, a simple constellation descended like syrup in the glowing dusk.

"Hello there. Hope you haven't been waiting long," my instructor called out cheerfully, as the polished propeller whistled to a stop. "Crikey, I've been rushing about delivering aircraft for the last couple of days; I'm absolutely whacked. But come on inside a moment, I've got something I need to tell you."

He unlocked the door to the Clubhouse where the hierarchy of furnishings had been restored.

"So, how was last night? Did you have some fun?" he asked.

"Well - it was certainly an eye-opener," I replied.

I expected him to settle back into his chair with the same mandarin demeanour. But, instead, he perched right up on the edge; there was none of the constraint that sometimes lingered from facing down boys little older than myself.

"Anyway, I wanted to see you because I was in Southampton yesterday," he began at a trot. "I happened to call in on an old friend of mine who runs this small flying-boat operation. They've just started a new service down to Darwin, Australia. But he was telling me that the whole thing's looking a bit doubtful at the moment because one of his pilots has gone down with something nasty – probably picked up in the tropics. The long and short of it is that this poor chap's not going to recover in time and, of course, he asked me whether I knew anyone who might be up for the job. I remembered what you said about being short of cash and thought you might be interested."

He stopped abruptly and then stared at me with a slight nod, as if I were a parrot that wouldn't talk.

"It really is a great opportunity," he went on. "especially with so few flying jobs around. It'll probably be great fun as well and, who knows, they might take you on permanently. So what do you think?"

"You mean - are they offering me a job?" I asked hesitantly. "As an airline pilot?"

"Well, you haven't got the job yet, but you're at the head of the queue, if you want it."

"Well, I'm certainly very flattered," I uttered, before breaking out into a rash of snags. "But when are they due to depart?"

"The day after tomorrow."

"The day after tomorrow," I said, almost laughing in

disbelief. "but I'll never get my pilot's licence by then."

"Well you'd only be the co-pilot, they hardly do any of the flying. It'll just be on-the-job training, that's all. You'd learn all the things that I've only touched upon - you know like navigation, night flying and that sort of thing."

"But I don't know anything about flying-boats or seaplanes. I've only ever flown a trainer."

"Listen," he said, reaching inside his jacket. "you're going to have to keep quiet about certain things. Don't worry, though, I've made some notes here about landing on water. But there's really nothing to it. I've also padded out your flying record a little."

He handed me a small notebook and I quickly thumbed through the pages, eager to see how my career would pan out.

"Come on. I thought you'd be jumping for joy," he continued in a disciplined funk. "I wouldn't do this for anyone, especially a student pilot. But you have a real feel for things. You've also got an excellent understanding for all the mechanical gubbins. You'll have no problem doubling up as a flight engineer. Opportunities like this only come up once in a blue moon. Damn it, I'm almost tempted to take the job myself."

He then looked at me intensely until his belief in me seemed to be assayed in streaks across his scalp.

"This way," he went on, smiling firmly, "you can carry on flying and, at weekends, you can still keep your hand in here with the Auxiliaries. Quite frankly, the RAF needs to hang onto people like you."

"Alright, if you think I'm up to it. I'll give it a go." I said finally, hoisting half a smile.

"Great," he said, clapping his hands together. "Hop on a train to Southampton tomorrow and talk it over. But, remember, you haven't actually got the job yet, so go away and study what I've written there and don't go selling yourself short," he warned. "I've done most of the donkey work already – so don't let me down."

8

There was something familiar waiting for me on the platform the next morning. It awoke with a squeal as the perambulating hiss emerged from its purple, grey bloom. The driver tried soothing the engine with a bruising polish and yet more coppered tonic; but I climbed aboard nursing an unpleasant sense of deja vu.

I had resolved to spend the journey double-checking my instructor's notes, repeating the lines over and over until the story didn't sound too bad. But I hadn't allowed for a Bank Holiday weekend and my studies were soon interrupted by legions of seasiders. With embarrassed smiles, they waddled on board in their factory boots, laden to the gunnels with lunchboxes and bottles tightly sealed to last the journey. They squeezed themselves onto the wooden benches and sat patiently sweltering in their heavy suits and collarless shirts, which collapsed over their pale bodies like wet cardboard. Time and again I retrieved toys from beneath the seat, while our smogged wanderings led us toward the coast. But, at the first glimpse of the regimented rows on the beaches, there was only blasphemous prose about the futility of it all.

The iron stalactites of Southampton station drifted slowly past like seaweed and the flanges choked to a halt on their liquorice rails. I stood back against the wall of the Waiting Room, while parents were pulled like a truss by their little people. They trampled forward, panting wildly, dribbling chocolate and confectionery they'd looted from the kiosk. When the ruck had cleared, I dug out the directions I had been given and set off toward the quiet cranes and loading yards.

I negotiated my way into a street behind the quayside which was lined with an uneven row of workshops. Being a Bank holiday, I didn't expect there to be much activity; but the calls of artisans railing against deadlines, tolled from pegged windows. I peered in to see sheets of buffed duralumin and sections of fuselage being wheeled about like scenery. They sat waiting by wings flushed with rivets, as mechanics applied grease guns to sultry engines through a multitude of nipples.

At the far end, a hangar tallied with the description I'd been given. 'EMPIRE AIR SERVICES' was proudly splashed across two vast concertina doors. The words strained with an authority that promised to be prolific around the world; but, as I stepped inside, my footsteps slapped bare walls. Yards of empty shelving watched as a couple of ladders leaned to one side dressed up like clothes horses. They stood awaiting the return of long-departed airliners whose oily shadows stained the floor.

There was a slipway leading down to the water, where one elderly flying-boat was still tethered to a small pier. It sat bobbing up and down on the tide, gently lifting its tail to anyone who might come too near. It dared my unshakeable inadequacy to run away like loo-roll; but, as I motioned slowly forwards, a figure hurtled out of a wooden office, perched on mezzanine stilts in the corner. He raced outside and shouted at two men who were crawling about on the wing. They both turned to look at him while he performed a song-and-dance on the pier. It didn't seem to make much difference however; when his display was over he tore back up the stairs and they continued in the same tempo, like monkeys on a bandstand.

Accompanied by their glum percussion, I ascended the stairs to the office where I could hear desperate voices muttering and heels stabbing the floor. At the open doorway, I looked in on a pair of lop-sided faces stretching out over a map. They were biting down on pencils through an ill-tempered haze of cigarettes and uppers; but there was also an unlikely hint of cologne, which was the only remnant of the glamour still being portrayed in the adverts on the walls.

I waited with all my answers at the end of a deep breath but no one looked up, until a telephone was slammed down behind the door.

"Damn it! There's no bloody answer." Snarled a woman in a blue uniform, as she swept across the floor. "This is no good. We'll have to think of something else. Have another look through this."

She dropped a telephone directory in front of the two men hovering over the map and all their papers flew up like feathers in a chicken coup. But their gaze was fixed upon me standing in the doorway and the woman immediately swung around.

"Can I help you?" She demanded beneath a hood of

perspiration.

"Yes, I'm sorry to disturb you." I replied "I'm looking for a Mr Hammond."

"*Mr* Hammond." She stated flatly. "There's no Mr Hammond here. I'm Ms Hammond, if that's who you want."

"Possibly. Yes. I was sent here by Wing Commander Canares."

I expected her to brighten up a little at the mention of my instructor's name. But she simply stared at me like an imposing damask. Her pursed lips shone scarlet in the gloom and my stance began to waver when the telephone suddenly rang. I waited for Ms Hammond to answer it; but she remained as if cast in marble, detached from a frieze that had quietly crept away.

"I understand you're looking for a pilot." I finally uttered with some desperation.

"Yes we are. But I wasn't expecting anyone."

"Did no one tell you I was coming?"

"No, I'm afraid not. I mean I saw Alec for a short while yesterday but he's just a friend of the family. We didn't talk about anything much."

She then looked round at her ink-pot genies and pulled her fingers through her hair as if it were rigging.

"Oh, I know what's happened," she drummed in a low voice, "I'll bet he's been round to the house. You can be sure my father's told him the mess we're in. They probably had a bloody good laugh."

She failed to unlock even the slightest emotion from their sewn-up faces and the burgeoning files behind them simply looked on, bound by string. Ms Hammond touched the sides of her head again, as if she were patting down gunpowder; she then turned back toward me like a portrait pulled from cold-store.

"So you've heard we're short of a pilot and you want the job, is that it?" she asked.

"Yes, that's it." I replied.

"Well, I suppose if Alec Canares sent you, you must be pretty competent."

She stepped forward and stared at me with large, forceful eyes that drooped slightly at the corners, as if damning me with faint praise.

"Welcome aboard," she said half-heartedly shaking my hand. "Be here tomorrow at 6 o'clock on the dot. The passengers embark at eight. Now if you can excuse me we're rather tied up trying to get our supply depots organised."

Without any further qualifications, she returned to her two-man cabal and I stood for moment, stunned by the apparent worth of my simply worded provenance.

"By the way," she asked, as I was reversing out of the room. "Do you have any engineering experience?"

Tractors and combines probably weren't what she had in mind - but delving into details clearly wasn't the order of the day.

"Well, I've carried out a number of engine rebuilds," I

said, after a pause.

"Oh good. That'll be very useful. We'll see you tomorrow."

9

Distant, anonymous Southampton now became twinned with Arcadia, as I quick-stepped back to the railway station. A smile smeared across my face and the train hurried away with telegraph poles can-canning past across a postcard sky. For once, I had beaten all my expectations and there was nothing to mourn - and nothing to topple on top of me on a dreary, Sunday afternoon.

My barricade of boxes welcomed me back into my room, seemingly teetering with anticipation. They watched in a reassuring silence as I stood wondering what I ought to take with me. Having unearthed my frayed canvas knapsack, I was ready to fill it with monsoon coats, mosquito nets, dry rot tablets and offerings for the gods. But, as I pulled it open, the smell of its innards kindled warm recollections of hiking, fishing and other carefree afternoons - which were still only touch-dry.

I hadn't planned to inform the remains of my family as to my whereabouts; but I gazed out of the window questioning my judgement. Perhaps I should have sounded a little more saddened when informed of my father's demise; but it had been as if my tutor were reading it from an old newspaper. A few months earlier I had heard the doctor quietly passing sentence upon us all through a blancmange of heavy doors and quilted curtains.

"Come on Doc. You can tell me the worst of it," my father had demanded. "For God's sake, sit down and have another sherry."

"No, Claude, I'm not spending an evening arguing with you about the diagnosis. I've written it all down. Everything you need to know. And don't open that envelope until I'm out the door."

Our doctor spoke with the authority of an ormolu clock; his measured consideration always appearing out-of-place in our house. I watched through the staircase spindles as he moved quietly across the hall, taking care not to crack the black-and-white flagstones sitting inches thick beneath his feet. He bowed beneath the blazing fanlight and drifted away in his slim, little Riley - leaving my father's Lagonda wobbling on its springs like a nesting hen.

At dinner that evening there was a nauseating polarity as I watched my brothers riding pillion. They sat willing my father to speak but he didn't so much as blink; any remarks they could manage were supplemented by nothing more than my mother's thoughtful pauses. Her eyes blindly fingered the walls as his clothes hung from his thinning frame; very soon tinned food and wooden sleep had replaced the carnal spirits that so often furnished the house. Voices dwindled to a whisper and there was a clash of glances every time one of them staked their claim to a greater share of the grief. I was only too glad to escape this growing draft of hysteria, among the repeated episodes of woolly students and yawning trees.

When my tutor summoned me to his study, I sat bowing to ceremony, before leaving a cheque and an unrequited goodbye with my neighbour. The railway signals waved goodbye to me forever, as I settled back into a first-class compartment. I sat totalling all the hours spent holding court with the labourers, who washed over the land every year like the tide. I was quite sure that prudence had prevailed over a pair of spivs, who had spent a lifetime looking for yet another excuse to dress up.

All the acres strewn with my resources and the views no one wanted accompanied me on the walk from the railway station. I approached the house expecting to be met by the flat-cap sighs of agrarian organs. But its spectacled mansards were busy sight-reading a scene on the driveway: a brace of wagons were busily evicting paintings and furniture from buttoned-up rooms that had always been spoken to. Amid the off-the-cuff comments, my brother stood like a bitter kernel, trying to extract some order from the dismay. He stood barking out orders that no one heard, while my mother loitered just inside the door like an unwanted bouquet.

"Oh hello darling. This is an unexpected surprise," she said fondling the mantelpiece in a once-silvered hall. "Have you come to collect some of the books your father left you? I suppose they'll be a big help for your studies. We're just moving them out of the drawing- room because Herbert wants a bit more space in which to work. The bookcases are also yours, you know. I've always thought those bookcases look so grand in any setting. You can tell these gentlemen where you'd like them to go."

She beamed out from a fragrant past when all my fragile efforts had been sniffed at. But nothing could precipitate a charade of appreciation or ruin my sense of legitimacy. I left behind a lifetime's supply of shaving paper and the cosy sounds of so many staff. It was only their plight that now dressed me down with any sympathy, as I pictured the house being ripped apart rind first.

I traipsed downstairs toward the telephone and stood with embarrassed demure; I waited for either a familiar voice or to be informed of the faltering price of life.

"Oh, it is so good to hear from you again. It has been such a long time since we have seen you."

Bertrand had been with our family for as long as I could remember. He and Renata, his wife of a thousand years or so, had joined the household sometime during the War. They had only intended to stay for the duration. But their plans to return to France were scuppered by a lengthy petition, gathered by myself and my brothers. A candid interest had always stoked his being; but now he was talking to me in short bursts - as if a long line of people were waiting to use the 'phone.

"I am afraid that your dear mama has gone to the Lakes," he confessed without being asked. "And neither of your brothers tell me where they are going these days. There have been quite a few changes here since your dear papa left us."

There was then a muffled disturbance on the line as if a scuffle had broken out. A voice came on which, for me, held more sway than any of the local constabulary; and sure enough, Renata was soon singing like bird.

"Bonjour mon cheri! C'est tellement merveilleux de vous entendre! Are your studies going well and did you get the pâté I sent you? I would have sent you some of those little patisserie you like so much as well; mais par bleu, que de difficultes. Now that your dear papa has gone. Dieu donne le repose a son ame. I suppose you have heard?"

"No. No one's told me anything. I only called to see how you were both keeping." I replied. "But I haven't had my allowance for a few months so I was wondering if maybe something was up."

"Oh mon Dieu. It has been terrible here. All the staff have left and your dear mama, when she is here, she just stays in her room. She is so upset with your dear brother, Master Neville, because he has been fighting over your dear papa's will. Combien il a change. He is wasting money on expensive solicitors and they march in here like an army, like the Germans, with no regard for anyone. And your dear brother, Master Herbert, is doing nothing. In fact we don't see him. He is always in London and myself and Bertrand have not received any wages for two weeks. But I can not believe that you have not had your allowance. You always did so much. Making sure that things worked. Quel dommage. Tant pis.

C'est une honte."

As I replaced the receiver, there was no sense of triumph knowing that the opinion I held of my siblings had been correct; Bertrand and Renata deserved better than to have their lives discarded by lawyers and the other gaming professions. But they were anonymous next to the ornamentation and artwork; indistinct from the livestock, except for a gated happiness that a life of loyal, dogged service should have locked shut.

10

With my funds all but exhausted, I spent that evening promenading about Southampton, courting captive landladies. Beneath goading lights, they cracked open their doors and shunned my advances, brandishing honky-tonk ivories. Only when I happened to mention that I was a pilot, was there any room for negotiation. I was eventually shooed upstairs without my dinner and I lay down in the darkness with nothing left to feed the meter.

Keen to avoid breakfast, I arrived at the hangar early the following morning and was greeted by the same distended echo; a mechanic was still savaging the flying-boat outside with dull blows. He was balanced on the propeller like a blacksmith on a trapeze, while his mate applied a bold new coat of silver paint to the fuselage.

I hadn't been given any Pilot's Notes, so was desperate to familiarise myself with the machine. I stepped along the pier and surveyed a flimsy forked-tail at one end and a pug-ugly nose at the other. It was a design itching with compromises, simply held together by an arboretum of struts and bracing wires; these reached up from an outrigger to a vast parasol wing, where two large radial engines were displaying their cylinder-heads like gargoyles.

Peering into the passenger cabin, I expected the aircraft to redeem itself with portaled views of luxury. But, instead, I was met by an ill-tempered smell of damp newspapers and tailored privilege suffering in the heat. The cabin was little better than a potting shed: exposed girders held up laddered luggage nets, while eight pairs of seats hastily hid their bald patches with a freshly-plucked doily. As I moved up the aisle, the carpet blushed with the patina of withered grass, seemingly shrinking at the thought of yet more fiery destinations where only hardwoods thrive.

The business end of the aircraft was separated from the passenger cabin by a thin piece of curtain. There was a diminutive galley to one side, where a carpet sweeper was watching over a hot water urn and two rows of aluminium cupboards. The door to the cockpit was closed and I knocked on it a couple of times, before presenting myself to a daunting abundance of wheels, levers, switches and dials; they sat blooming in puddles of hydraulic fluid beneath an all-enveloping glass canopy. It was a far cry from the controls of the jolly yellow plaything that used to entertain me if conditions were near-perfect.

Hesitantly, I leaned forward between the two pilots' seats and was, at first, a little overwhelmed by the confusion of bakelite and ironmongery. But, after a time, I managed to decipher all the basic controls and I stepped back outside feeling somewhat reassured. It may have seen better days but it was, at least, a fairly honest liner, which was unlikely to spring too many surprises on a novice pilot like me.

The mechanic was still re-mortgaging the carburettors

with filed-down parts, as I emerged from the shadow of the wing. I glanced up toward him but he stared straight through me with bovine eyes, stirred by fatigue. I knew how engines could be prone to tantrums, no matter how often they were rubbed, fed or tickled. I was about to offer him some assistance when Ms Hammond came skipping down the stairs from her office.

"Good morning," she said, with her coins and keys jangling like sleigh bells in her pockets. "The passengers will be here very soon, so put your things on board the plane. You'll find a couple of spare uniforms in the stowage compartment to the rear. Hopefully one of them should fit you. At least try them for size."

She twinkled with a fickle sprinkling of cosmetics but beneath the thin, coach-line of mascara, it didn't look as though she'd had much sleep. As soon as she'd finished with me, her faint smile disappeared and she turned on the mechanic working above us. As I withdrew inside the plane, there was a quiet volley of profanities between them; sounds I was well-used to hearing when an engine is reluctant to start up.

Next to a small WC at the stern, I unearthed a cap and a tunic which, fortunately, matched the trousers I was already wearing. I gave all the buttons a quick polish before straightening up - just as Miss Hammond entered the cabin. I wasn't looking for marks out of ten; but she barely broke from a manly stride that had the floor flexing like toffee beneath her feet. Being still largely ignorant of procedures, I chased her up the aisle and watched from the cockpit door, as she began running through a list of pre-flight checks.

"Can you go and wait by the entrance gate," she said spinning around. "You'll need to show the passengers on board and help put their luggage away."

"Do you have a list of the passengers' names?" I postured delicately.

"Well, it's in my office. But, don't worry about it," she snapped. "It's not as if there's any room on board for stowaways."

I had few preconceptions about how airlines operated, but I had assumed that the pilot, or even the co-pilot, would enjoy a certain status. Despite my brazen new outfit, however, I was beginning to feel like something of an apparition. I clearly lay a long way below Ms Hammond in the ranks; exactly where was difficult to ascertain because I had yet to meet any other members of the crew.

Things only started to became a little clearer as I waited alone at the entrance gate. The mechanic approached pushing a large luggage trolley that hissed like a goose robbed of its quack.

"Stick all the luggage on that and then give me a shout," he said gruffly, wiping silver paint off his hands.

I gave him a smile, but it didn't seem to make much difference. He returned to the aircraft as it basked beneath a taunting circle of seagulls. The new paint job had done nothing for its appearance and it sat stewing in the water like a second-hand slipper bath. It certainly bore no resemblance to the latest Empire-class flying-boats being offered by the likes of *Imperial Airways*. Nor was it likely to impress a clientele that would probably consist largely of society marriages and slayers of the apostrophe.

As the first of them began to arrive, all I could do was turn up my smile and become deaf to their impending drill of judgement. Like a modern masquerade, they rolled up aboard taxis and swanky, enamelled galleons running with buxom fenders: a spectrum of mayfly prosperity and primrose wealth brimmed beneath hair piece salads and barnet desserts. Mouthpiece husbands unhorsed shoulder-pad wives that had been traded to keep regiments well-stocked and waiting lists out of reach. They emerged in a delicate cuticle of easy-to-swallow pieces, before floating slowly towards me as I stood ready to lick off their make-up.

Others, however, were simply lucky to be at table, shaking the dice: disastrous ensembles appeared in a flurry of handkerchiefs and dusty plumage, like foxes chasing away the gulls. They marched toward the plane, wielding inflections that could give you a headache; and, invariably, they were followed closely behind by a eunuch uddered by day baggage.

Standing at the end of the pier, Miss Hammond corralled them like a queue at a labour exchange, before attempting to cram them into the plane. But they all seemed to have something to say and they gathered around her with the same doggedness that gypsies and barrow boys learn in the womb. One by one, she dispelled them with guarantees from A to Z, while flashing a big grin. Her face then creased in frustration as she signalled abruptly for me to bring forth the luggage.

"Hurry up, for God's sake, will you," she scowled. "We should have left 10 minutes ago."

I pushed the trolley along the pier and began passing the suitcases to the mechanic, who appeared at a small hatch near the waterline. The aircraft swayed impatiently as he carefully distributed the load evenly along the keel. I stretched out my hand to thank him when, finally, he emerged from the hull - but there was no poignant send-off. He released the mooring lines as soon as I had stepped off the pier and then sauntered off with his reddened face throbbing like a sore.

Inside the passenger cabin, I negotiated my way slowly up the aisle, as if fashioning a new dance. I always had a sense of anticipation before any take-off and I expected to see all the passengers gripped by the same ballooning excitement. But, having furnished their darling cricket with a newspaper, peregrine grey men sat perfectly oblivious to the plight of their secretary birds; these poor creatures waddled about in front of me struggling with vanity cases, seemingly disabled by impossible shoes and gloved paws. When they finally took to their seats, the horsehairs in the seat cushions ruined their dressage; they joined a fidgeting choir of fading Gerties and Berthas, who had been reduced by the squeeze to just an ill-fitting pair of curtains.

The passengers were finally brought to heel when Miss Hammond emerged from the flight deck. I stood to attention next to her, halfway inside the galley.

"Good morning ladies and gentlemen." She began in a good, singing voice, "Welcome aboard..."

It was an animated address for an audience that sat arranged like photographs. She promised postcard weather all the way to Darwin and listed all the stops we would be making en route; I tried dotting them across the globe but lost her somewhere in the Indian subcontinent. She then went on to describe the aircraft and its features and, at that point, I expected her to introduce us both by name. But we were simply passed off as 'the crew' - which left me still unsure as to my exact position.

Once we had taken our bows, I loitered at the back of the cockpit like an ass, while Miss Hammond fiddled at the navigator's station.

"Shall I sit down, Miss Hammond?" I finally coughed up with my hand on the co-pilot's seat.

"Well, where else were you planning to sit?" She replied. "And you can stop calling me 'Miss Hammond'."

"So, how would you like me to address you?"

"You don't have to address me as anything," she growled, clambering into the Captain's chair. "If you've got something to say then just say it. After the engines have fired up I won't be able to hear you anyway."

"Perhaps it would help if I put these on," I said lifting up a pair of headphones hanging on the control column.

"I wouldn't bother, they don't work," she muttered dismissively.

She then dragged a large map out from under her seat and she dropped it onto my lap like a hearth rug.

"Here, hang on to that. I've marked on our flight path. When we're off the water, keep an eye on our progress. Make sure we don't stray too far off course."

I'd had a few lessons in navigation but I couldn't begin to decipher a score of pencil lines tabulated by tea rings; more importantly, I couldn't remember where we were supposed to be heading and Miss Hammond seemed too busy with the starting procedure to humour my glowing ignorance.

"Now don't touch any of the controls," she warned, pointing loosely to an apothecary of dials in front of me. "Just watch all those engine gauges and make sure everything stays dead centre. The port motor's been giving a little trouble lately, so let me know if it starts running hot."

The cruel gaze of monocles took me miles away from whatever else she may have said. I sat motionless at the helm in a slightly mortified haze, no longer filling in the middle or pulling up the rear. She offered me some cotton wool like communion on a long pole; but I politely declined knowing, that as her newly-appointed flight-engineer, I'd be using my ears as much as anything else.

She slowly stirred each propeller and the engines

awoke in a boom of smoke and hammed fists. All the pins and needles began to throb, laughing off my efforts as I sat deafened by the sound of cold ugly anomalies. She gunned the sniffing spinners and eased us away from the pier, taking care not to flood the carburettors with anything too sudden. We motored out into the harbour where she paused only to check the trim tabs against the flags on the quayside.

With the nose yawing listlessly, she braced the control column in one sinuous span, before releasing a motive yell; it grabbed me by the scruff of the neck and thrust me back into my chair. We gathered speed like a monk hitching up his habit; blinding perspiration burnished the canopy as we thumped along in jolts that left me winded. The crisp white rollers of Southampton Water goaded and toyed with Miss Hammond until she wrenched back on the column, heaving on it like bellows. The aircraft leaned back on its haunches and, in a sequinned blaze and a blizzard of rice, we finally broke from the water's suck with a fit of twitching flaps and creaking rivets.

11

I couldn't help but smile as the aircraft clawed toward the clouds; I peered across at the wings shrugging off the water clinging to its skin. It ran like rats, falling away toward bearded vessels dragging their barnacled bellies through a caustic surf. They fumed from their smokestacks, seemingly reaching up with dirty hands imprisoned within just two dimensions.

As we crossed the coast of France, I looked down through the side screen and tried sight-reading the map. I fumbled for bearings using any arteries and landmarks -but the crooked green bocage looked the same in every direction. The scything scream of the propellers seemed to malign my efforts, crippling my concentration and, soon, they were joined by a darkening horizon that began to smother my view of the ground.

Stooled formations gathered around us and soiled the sky. They contorted like candles and the aircraft began to buck in Miss Hammond's hands as the wind broke against the sides. It undid her carefully embroidered adjustments and she struggled to subdue the machine. I sat ready to reach out and join her grasp at the controls but her eyes remained fixed at Full Ahead.

She sat like an ever-quickening piano player, while I rolled around in my seat. The rain snapped against the canopy, keeping time as it dripped down onto me through the glass above my head.

"Go and check on the passengers, would you?" Ms Hammond finally bellowed amid the withering din.

She looked slightly deranged in the half-light and, for a moment, I sat restrained by the seatbelt's bite. I was reluctant to leave her, wrestling with the bear outside. But one final glare threatened to rip the braid from my sleeves, so I took my crumpled gallantry out into the passenger cabin.

I drew back the curtain and slowly processed down the aisle like a feeble chaplain, wholly relieved that I had skipped breakfast. As the plane keeled about in the swell, churning bodies sat lashed together with clasped hands. Only a handful of faces still endured, amid a pitiful gloom that seemed to be hanging almost lifeless from their spectacle chains. A spirited salute was the only relief I could administer and some managed to eke out faux smiles, like trophy heads mounted on spikes. But for the most part, buttoned-down outfits simply glanced up from biting the carpet. As I tip-toed through the retching herd, one of these managed to reach out and grab me by the arm.

"Excuse me. Are you going to be serving any refreshments?" a tweedy gent called out, leaning across his stricken wife.

"Is there something you'd like?" I replied, crouching down next to him.

"Well, I think we could all do with a drink."

"I'll – I'll see what I can do," I stuttered.

I staggered back to the cockpit and reported to Miss Hammond with my hands megaphoned around my snout.

"Some of the passengers would like a drink. They're looking a bit worse for wear." I shouted.

"OK. See to it," she answered without turning round. "Take whatever you can find in the galley."

My experience as a waiter went little beyond serving sherry at Christmas and, looking about the galley, I wasn't encouraged by the slow clapping of the cupboard doors. It simply revealed a trembling huddle of cloudy tumblers and very limited assortment of alcohol. Furthermore, with the weather worsening, I began to suspect that my predecessors had worked their passage for Ms Hammond, having run away from a circus. The plane pulled on my collar like a choke chain and I could barely stay upright, even when holding myself between the cupboards.

Nevertheless, I began serving the drinks in a series of relays. The passengers either yelled out their orders as if it were some sort of blood sport; or else, I was forced to lip-read colourless voids that emitted just curdled breaths. Some smiled, lightly entertained as I swayed down the aisle. But at the rear of the cabin, where the fog of tobacco hung like hemp, one or two still bit down hard on decorum.

"Your Campari and soda, madam," I said handing a tumbler to a buoyant trifle.

She took the glass but simply held it out in front of her,

as though it were attracting flies. I peered into it, unable to see the problem until her travelling companion rested his crossword and gave the mix a stir with his pen. He then tapped it against the side like a conductor's baton and normal service was resumed.

I then moved on to the final row, where a pair of haughty grandees were perched like reptiles soaking up the sun: another loyal coaxial summoned their drinks in a once-glorious suit that was now curling like a leaf at the lapels. His wife remained quietly emblazoned in costume brooches and clasps, that were struggling to hold her in. She sat perfectly still, staring at my badge until I placed her glass in front of her.

"Excuse me, young man," she suddenly burst like a blunderbuss. "If you are the pilot who, may I ask, is flying the plane at this moment?"

I almost choked on the smell of her talcum powder; but her embittered gaze was vaguely familiar. I'd seen it sniping over tea and sneering through the railings at débutante balls. She chanted an anthem that was proudly ignorant of all things mechanical and I quickly glanced up the aisle to make sure I'd closed the cockpit door.

"Oh don't worry madam," I replied, taking care not to spit. "We're being flown by the automatic pilot."

"In this weather?" her limp companion chipped in, with some validity. "Isn't that rather foolhardy?"

"I can assure you, sir, this aircraft is fitted with the very latest device. It's absolutely safe." I persevered. "In fact, it can probably fly the plane better than I could in these conditions."

They both swallowed my nonchalance like a gobstopper; but I withdrew with a commanding step that was impossible to catch. I detached my smile and left it on the tray in the galley, before staggering back to the haven of the cockpit. Miss Hammond was still rigidly refusing the aircraft's drunken manoeuvrings and she drove on grim-faced, as if the counterpoint of the engines were dictating her destiny.

12

I continued hanging onto my seat as we bounded over the crests and bumps like a steeplechaser; there was little else for me to do, except watch grey reeds raking past the windows. Ms Hammond remained anchored next to me, with only a sprig of hair betraying her exertions; each time it popped out from behind her ear she quickly brushed it back, cursing it like a parrot on her shoulder.

We both scrutinized the weave on the horizon, trying to peer through it until, eventually, a slow yawn appeared. It broke through the bearded darkness to reveal a benign willow pattern ahead of us. Its scanty wisps beckoned like best wishes from a peace pipe and Ms Hammond reclined a little into her seat.

"Better check on the passenger cabin again," she called out, looking at her watch.

I didn't relish the thought of another run-in with any of the passengers. But I was too hoarse to answer with anything except a nod. Having poured myself a glass of water in the galley, I simply peered into the passenger cabin through a crack in the curtain. The less seasoned travellers were now dozing cheek to cheek, while the pipe-smoking veterans at the rear played with their box cameras. The Blunderbuss, however, still sat with her stranglehold on civility, making disdainful glances at her peers as they hobbled past her to get to the WC. Her salty deportment was chiselled into place, confirming all my initial prejudices. There seemed no sense in antagonising her any further, so I returned to the cockpit, taking with me a glass of water for Ms Hammond.

She looked a little bewildered as I gingerly presented it to her; and instead of taking the glass, she reached down under her seat and handed me a Thermos flask. Whatever concoction was inside, certainly looked and smelled rather bullish; but she sipped it tenderly, until the ubiquitous features of a dockyard began puncturing the skyline.

She throttled back and we slowly circled above a sunlit constellation sprinkled across the harbour's face. I glanced down at the map and surmised that it was probably Marseilles. Miss Hammond handed me her cup and began pulling on various levers, which set the aircraft on a gentle glide path. With the engines chattering quietly in uneasy hiccups, she hoarded the controls in each hand and we side-slipped past the harbour jaws.

The moment we licked the surface, the water grabbed us like gum; it washed over the bow, kicking and foaming against the hull. The aircraft ploughed on, hissing and snorting buckets until we finally settled into the surf. When the mist had cleared, cranes and corroded vessels towered over us, welcoming us like a mongrel. Their closed ranks ran like a bronzed phalanx, holding back a mob of harshly-profiled warehouses; these seemed to have muscled their way past the shuttered natives, which now stood gazing forlornly with their elegant facades peeling in the sun.

Miss Hammond leaned the aircraft round and we taxied toward a jetty, where a Force 9 squint stood proudly exposed to the naval. He carefully guided her approach while she worked the throttles like a rudder.

"Good old Pierre, I knew I could depend upon him," she muttered wearily, as the nose nudged the timbers.

She then looked uncomfortably toward me, before thrusting her head out through the side screen. There was a stifled groan and I watched, at the mercy of any number of pompous platitudes, as she puked up over the side.

"Can you see to the passengers please," she garbled, waving me away with her handkerchief.

I got up slowly from my seat but, once again, felt caught in an auction - between solid subservience and some rather more flighty sentiments. As the propellers wind-milled to a stop, all I could hear were Ms Hammond's laboured breaths cratering the seat cushions.

"Go on will you, please," she said looking round as I waited by the cockpit door. "And make sure everyone leaves the plane."

She then buried her face in her hands and I reluctantly made another curtain call, in front of an audience that was similarly discoloured. I crabbed up the aisle, doffing my cap before offering my hand at the door. The passengers staggered out of the plane in an almost festive display: gripping the chairs, stroking the walls or hanging onto one another's tails.

They gaggled on the pier, devoid of almost all cosmetic coordination; most were nursing heads that were now a burden instead of a piece and their outsized collars flapped about like loose bandages in the breeze.

The Blunderbuss was one of the last to leave but she proudly stopped in front of me, as if balancing a ball on her snout.

"And would you mind telling us how long we have before departure?" she demanded.

"I suppose - an hour or so," I replied.

"And where do you recommend we should go?"

"Well, would you, perhaps, like to get a spot of lunch somewhere?" I suggested.

"If the next leg of the journey's going to be anything like the last, I don't think we ought to risk it," the tweedy gent piped up from coddling his wife. "Do you have the latest weather report?"

"No I'm afraid not," I confessed.

"Well we could both do with something, even if its only a cup of tea," Campari and Soda added. "But you've clearly not been to Marseilles before because there isn't a decent restaurant anywhere in this place."

They both looked awkwardly toward me and the Blunderbuss loitered just inside in the doorway, as if teething through the soles of her feet. A well-tanned colonial, standing immediately behind her, then leaned in over her shoulder; he had spent most of the flight fast asleep and, apart from having his feet in the aisle, he had caused me no trouble whatsoever. Now, however, his dusky companion appeared keen to nurture the Blunderbuss's despondency.

"Excuse me for interrupting, madam," He said in a long, slow drag, "but I know a delightful hotel just a short walk from here. It has a charming little brasserie which looks out onto the basilica. I'm sure you'd quite like it."

The Blunderbuss seemed startled by his brazen proposition and she looked round sharply to scrutinise his tailoring.

"I'm not sure if some of these poor people are capable of walking," she puffed, pointing through the doorway.

"Well if it's any comfort, I have some marvellous new air sickness pills. They really work wonders. But it's best not to have them on empty stomach."

He glanced generously outside at the minted grazing on the pier and invited the Blunderbuss to join him under the shade of the wing. There he gathered the passengers together like a plutocracy of accents, while I looked on, feeling as though he were about to be shot from a cannon. But, with his arms outstretched, he swathed them all in the club spirit they were craving and quickly dispelled the quarrelsome stench. He then led them away, seemingly divining for everything they asked for, such as cocoa and grandiose commodes. I watched in amazement until they disappeared amid the parade of fleshpots and saloons lining the quayside.

There seemed an equal chance that, perhaps, Ms Hammond might want me to join her for a cup of tea somewhere; so I waited patiently on the pier, surrounded by drums of petroleum which had all had their markings scratched out. I stood choking on the noxious distemper belching from Pierre's refuelling pump until, like a dishevelled cherub, he looked down from the top of the wing.

"Femmes. Les oublier. Les oublier," he sniggered, before blowing me a raspberry.

I smiled back and shrugged my shoulders as best I could but finally retreated back inside the aircraft. Ms Hammond was still on the flight deck, deep in conference with a compact, strenuously pinking and pulling at her features.

"By the way," she said spinning round, snapping her box shut. "I don't know who else you've worked for but on this airline you're to keep things ship-shape. Do you understand?"

She swept past me and threw back the curtain to the passenger cabin.

"Look at all this bloody mess. You can't just leave it like this. Everything has to be secure for landing and take-off. Pick up those glasses and make a start on the washing up. And, for God's sake, empty those sick pans, rinse them thoroughly outside. Goodness me, anyone would have thought we'd started serving porridge for breakfast. Now, if you can excuse me," she said treading carefully down the aisle. "I need to go and make a telephone call. Oh and by the way," she added at the door. "the lav's blocked. See to that as well."

The romance of flying-boat travel was certainly diminishing at a rate of knots. But 'mucking-in' had always been a part of my vocabulary; I took up my station by the sink in the galley and watched through the window as Ms Hammond diminished along the pier. I hadn't been reprimanded by such a shrill soprano since my schooldays, when Lady Houston had stepped up to the lectern in the Assembly Hall. She had berated us all like a rusticated general, banging a parasol that probably morphed into a shotgun.

"Look at me" she'd chanted. "I'm a 74 year old widow. I should be at home making jam and chutney. But I'm not. Tomorrow I'm going flying with the Duchess of Bedford. What are you lot going to be doing? You'll probably have your heads stuck in books, I shouldn't imagine. You should be up there - in the clouds." she scolded, pointing up to the ceiling.

Her brand of insanity was nothing short of intoxicating and after her departure, none of the speccy Crown Agents ever cut much of a figure. No one wanted to hear about a career governed by button-hole politics. Indeed, only the Bentley Boys rivalled her performance. They arrived on the day of the General Strike, having commandeered a fleet of double-decker buses. We swarmed around them and they roused us all with the rallying cry: 'Room for one more on top!'.

Knowing that I was satisfying that mantra, was cause

enough to smile. But, as I crouched down at the water's edge to empty the gozundas, the noise of Pierre's fuel pump was augmented by the rumble of aero-engines. I looked up and, in the distance, another much larger flying-boat appeared out of the clouds. It floated downwards with its flaps spread, casting a shadow that stained the water indigo. As it touched down there was none of the feral pantomime we had exhibited. The fuselage simply cleaved the surface and enchanting vortices were whisked up like cocktails from its wing tips.

As it turned to starboard, the words 'IMPERIAL AIRWAYS LONDON' fanned out across its flanks. I had seen their new Empire flying-boats depicted on posters. But I had assumed they were nothing more than renditions sketched by hopeless romantics. I couldn't believe an aircraft could offer facilities such as sleeping quarters and a smoking lounge. Now, however, as it crossed the harbour in front of me, the mighty Empire looked as big as a destroyer. Its four engines bristled like howitzers from the leading edge. Each one seemed to snarl with the combined omnipotence of a syndicated boardroom and the disdain of the Piccadilly clubs. I could almost see the devoted crew laughing in unison as they motored past and the bow wave left our ugly little troll thumping against the pier.

It eventually disappeared behind a line of terminated ships and, somewhat solemnly, I returned to the galley. I finished rendering everything perpendicular, just as Ms Hammond reappeared outside. She yelled up at Pierre, who clambered down onto the float; I then watched from the window as she proceeded to produce large amounts of money from various parts of her person. She counted it out into one thick wedge in front of him before handing it over. Her payment also included a couple of pecks on the cheek and some generous thanks – even though her French was far from expert. When she went on to ask him something about the luggage, matters quickly descended into a game of charades; so I quickly moved over to the doorway, ready to lend a hand.

"Did no one ask for their luggage before they left?" Ms Hammond enquired, finally looking toward me.

"No," I replied. "Were they supposed to?"

"A couple by the name of Beauchamp were leaving here for the Riviera apparently. Well, it's too bad if they don't want it," She muttered nonchalantly. "Right, time for a quickie ciggie," she said, pulling a silver cigarette case out from her pocket. "Do you smoke?"

"No, I'm afraid not," I replied.

Perhaps I was a little hasty with my answer because Pierre then graciously stepped up and gave her one of his roll-ups; I was left to watch from the side-lines while they stood together on the pier, sucking away in ecstasy until the passengers came into view.

Ms Hammond quickly discarded her butt and ushered Pierre back up on top of the wing. The well-tanned colonial was one of the first to return and I waited by the cabin door, ready to thank him for his earlier intervention. But he simply smiled at me, before stopping in front of Ms Hammond, just as she was about to disappear inside the plane.

"Goodness me, I hardly recognised you in that uniform," he said, slowly removing his sunglasses. "So it's true - you really have started chipping away at your old man's block."

Ms Hammond glanced up at his high-rise stature and seemed to miss a step.

"I don't remember seeing your name on the passenger list," she said coldly.

"No, it was a last minute thing," he said looking toward his dusky companion, who was stepping quietly inside the aircraft. "I managed to cadge a lift off an old friend of mine. She usually flies by Imperial Airways. But I told her that family and friends get a discount if they fly with you lot," he added with a wink.

"I'm sure," Ms Hammond replied, smiling obliquely at the other passengers as they trotted on board.

"So you got fed up with life on the stage did you?"

"Something like that."

"I must say, I'm rather surprised. I saw a glittering future for you in the West End," he said, smirking in my direction. "Maybe you'll be providing all the in-flight entertainment. A little bit of cabaret to keep everyone awake. Why don't you do that Max Miller song you used to sing for us. Proper little Marie Lloyd you were," he grinned.

"I hope you realise this isn't the service down to the

Cape." Ms Hammond snapped. "We're heading to Darwin."

"I'm well aware of that, my dear. But don't worry I'm only with you as far as Karachi. Then I'm catching a steamer across to Mombasa. So I'll soon be out of your hair."

"Well if you wouldn't mind getting on board now we're due to depart," Ms Hammond said firmly, showing him the door.

"Aye, aye Skipper," he said, giving her a salute.

He slipped inside the aircraft just as Pierre was reeling in his hoses. Ms Hammond thanked him once more before closing the door with a conspicuous thump. I followed her down the aisle but about halfway along, the Tweedy gent spun round in his seat with his face covered in grumble.

"Excuse me, stewardess," he said. "My wife and I have flown with Imperial Air Services many times before - we even know Mr Hammond, the owner. I trust he still owns the business?"

"Yes, sir, he does," Miss Hammond assured him.

"Well that's good to hear because he was always extremely amenable. But, I'm afraid, on this occasion, we haven't been allocated our usual seats."

"I am so sorry about that, sir. Would you perhaps like to sit over there?" Ms Hammond suggested, glancing across at the empty seats the Beauforts had occupied.

"That would be much better, thank you." the tweedy gent stated, without consulting his wife.

They then proceeded to change places and Ms

Hammond vanished behind the curtain. I was left stuck behind them in the aisle and, of course, it was only a matter of time before the Blunderbuss started to feel ignored.

"Excuse me," she said finally, tapping me on the arm with her claw. "I do hope there's going to be a meal served on this next part of the flight because we've had hardly anything to eat. The prices here in *Mar-sales* are absolutely scandalous. We had to pay 20 francs for a cup of tea and a sandwich. That's almost 2 shillings and 6 pence."

I shuddered at her pronunciation but bent down toward her with another smile wedged into my mouth.

"Rest assured, madam, we'll be serving refreshments once we're over the Mediterranean." I said with a powder puff promise.

"Thank you. I'll look forward to it and I hope the stewardess will be slightly less bashful by then."

She returned my grin with interest and, as soon as the Tweedy gent had transplanted his wife's belongings, I swept up the aisle. When I pushed through the curtain, however, I almost crashed into Ms Hammond who was standing just on the other side.

"Contemptible bugger." she muttered, spinning round and disappearing into the cockpit.

She sat down at the controls and began furiously throwing switches, while I pretended to look down at the map.

"Were you referring to me, just now?" I finally asked.

"What?" she said looking up. "Oh no, no. I was talking

about that sod and the dolled-up trollop he's sitting with. My God she must be twice his age."

"You mean the gentleman you were talking to on the pier?"

"He's no gentleman. If he wasn't my brother-in-law I wouldn't even give him and his sort the time of day," she fumed.

"I didn't know you were married." I remarked quietly.

"I'm not. He's married to my sister. Miserable waster. Him and the rest of that Happy Valley Set. Bloody pills and prescriptions that's what it's all about. The lousy bastard should have been struck off years ago."

I was unused to hearing quite so many profanities in such a short space of time, so swiftly referred back to the map.

"Is it Malta we're heading for now?" I asked, making a calculated guess.

"That's right. We'll be stopping there for the night. We've got about a seven hour flight ahead of us - so keep an eye on all those gauges. I want to make sure we get to Karachi without any mishaps. I don't want to look at that bloody smarmy mug of his any longer than I have to."

After that I chose not to say anything and left Ms Hammond to continue the starting procedure. But just as the starboard motor started turning, something else suddenly came to mind.

"By the way," I asked hurriedly. "Will we be serving a meal on this next leg of the flight?"

"Yes, you'll have to," she said without looking round. "There are some lunch boxes in the galley. It's not going to be a hot meal - I think there's some salad and bread rolls. It's a sort of Ploughman's. There's a menu somewhere in the galley. It's all written down there."

Her answer wasn't quite what I had been hoping to hear. However, as we taxied away, the sun was shining brightly; I felt sure the passengers would finally begin to enjoy the flight and all the spectacle it had to offer. Before opening the throttles, Ms Hammond looked across through the side screen, as if to wave to Pierre one last time. But he had already tottered away, doubtless to procure some more anonymous fuel drums, ready for the return leg of the trip.

13

The outlook was now girdled by just a hazy petticoat, embroidered with seabirds in lazy flight. The Mediterranean stretched ahead, encouraging us forward with gentle currents that patted the sides of the hull. The dull, serviceable colours that had washed over the canopy now gave way to triumphant fishing-boats; each one cheered us on as they busily trawled their claim.

At the controls, Miss Hammond remained as stiff as ever, entrenched in black and white. She sat scanning the dials and subduing the control column each time it jiggered in her hands. The motors played to her in a minor key, stamping down on any passion I still had for the mechanicals. They doled out their noise like a perpetual homebrew which soaked into my spine and numbed most of my senses.

None of the instruments pressed up against me anymore and the map was now redundant over the water. With the weather much calmer, there seemed a slim chance that she might entrust some of the flying to me. So, for an hour or so, I waited patiently, putting off any thought of serving more refreshments.

Eventually, however, Ms Hammond looked toward me, as if she had picked up some sort of odour. Instead of harping like a klaxon in my ear, she reverted to a mime derived from a courtesan age. A couple of deft hand movements sent me away to the galley where beverages were waiting to be distributed and the dinner needed to be prepared. I vacated my position as the co-pilot, flight-engineer and navigator and took up my station in the galley, as purser and sous-chef.

By now my cap badge had lost much of its shine and I felt wholly unsuited for work in the hospitality trade. I was quite content to let the passengers' voices shrivel up and their lips shrink bitterly as they suffered without a drink. Furthermore, there seemed to be no rush to ready the dinner; feeding time was still about four hours away and I didn't expect Ploughman's to present much of a challenge. But that was before I unearthed the ingredients stashed behind the door.

Instead of cleaned, sliced, pre-fabricated parts, I found crushed pork pies and misshapen vegetables, still covered in muck. As I stared down into each cardboard box, I quickly became zombied by a vision - where every superlative was hurled at me as soon as I stepped inside the passenger cabin. I simply couldn't face the same shriek of condescension which I had so often known at home. The antidote had always been Renata's soothing warble and, thanks to her culinary creativity, mealtimes were invariably a quiet occasion. No matter how poor the Summer or how strict the rationing during the War, her ornamental pastries never failed to transform even the most mundane pie; more particularly, her salads always entertained the eye - even when they were largely made up of flowers and hedgerow.

Anything I attempted along the same lines was bound to be a poor imitation. But, using just my pen-knife, I slowly began to arrange each serving. Greens that had been piled like silage were re-assembled with Bonsai precision. Any imperfections were whittled away until every tomato was a coronet and every carrot was mercilessly filleted. When my time was finally up, I checked under each lettuce leaf for any stray creepy-crawlies. I then proudly assembled each plate on my tray, ready for another performance.

I pushed through the curtain into the aisle as if emerging from a cape. But I was greeted by a camp of dead-pan faces, tapping their feet, waiting to be impressed. They had gobbled up the view and now sat handcuffed to their seats. A small number answered my smile but mostly they just stared down at my simple offering. Worse still, when I reached the Blunderbuss on the back row, it was clear that the calm weather had done nothing to settle her nerves.

"Once again I see we are being served by the pilot," she said puffing out her chest, as I placed her feed in front of her.

"I'm sorry madam, is there something you're not happy with?" I enquired.

"Yes, there is, as I've told you before, I think it's extremely dangerous, not to say improper, for the pilot to serve dinner while the stewardess hides in the kitchen."

"I assure you madam the aircraft is in a perfectly safe attitude."

"So you keep saying but I don't find your words very

reassuring. I mean, supposing we hit a sudden patch of turbulence, supposing an engine fails, supposing something breaks. There's little point in you busying yourself topping up the drinks and serving bread rolls if we're all hurtling to our deaths."

She was now quite red in the face and her trusty grandee tended to her disposition.

"Hear, hear!" he cried out in trigger-happy speech marks.

All around me heads slowly cranked as the cantankerous rot began to spread; so I assembled the remains of my flat-pack charm into one last crooked smile.

"Very well madam. I shall return to the cockpit and I hope you enjoy your meal."

But as I turned toward the flight deck an elderly lady sitting across the aisle tapped me on the arm.

"I'm sorry to trouble you young man," she said peering over her glasses, "I'm afraid there's a rather strong smell coming from the lavatory, I think perhaps it might be blocked."

"Unfortunately, madam," I said, cradling my voice in both hands, "I'll have to attend to it when we land as I must now resume my other duties."

I straightened myself up and walked briskly back to the cockpit, almost slamming the door behind me. For once I didn't so much as glance at Miss Hammond as I climbed back into my seat. I simply resumed my watch at the engineering panel, trying to reciprocate her apparent ambivalence.

14

It was now quite clear that the division of labour on board was more than just an irritation. But, most importantly, I had no idea how I was going to clear away the main course and start serving the pudding. I sat quietly brooding next to Ms Hammond, looking for a chance to raise the issue. But she remained wrapped in hieroglyphic profundity, wearing a face that could have sunk a thousand ships.

As the light began to fail, she perched on the edge of her seat, glaring into the darkness with her neck bent in the middle and her back bowed at full stretch. Every now and again she massaged the blood through her neck; but she never failed to hold the aircraft in strict submission. I glanced across a number of times trying to thaw out something resembling a smile - and then I offered to pour her a drink. But, as she passed me her flask, I made the mistake of switching on a small spotlight above my head.

"Turn that damn thing off!" She bawled.

Harsh, bony breath accompanied her cruel squint and the ecstatic spit from the exhaust flashed like lightening across her face. I wilted like a weed and there now seemed no way to head off the catalogue of complaints, sure to be waiting for us when we landed. But, as I sat with my constitution already crumbling, a faint, whimpering voice splashed into the engine noise behind us.

"Excuse me," the tweedy gent called out from the doorway. "Do you think someone could turn the lights on? It's awfully dark in the cabin."

I jumped out of my seat and spread my arms out like Moses.

"Yes, of course, sir," I said coaxing him like a goat out of the cockpit. "that's no problem at all."

The cabin lights were one of the few functions on the aircraft I knew how to operate because all the switches were in the galley.

"And when someone finally gets around to serving the tea and coffee," he added sharply. "I'll have a tea with one sugar and my wife will have a black coffee."

I gave him some empty assurances and switched on the cabin lights; but, short of donning a disguise, there seemed little else I could do. As he returned to his seat, however, I peered through the curtain and saw that the Blunderbuss and her sidekick had both fallen asleep. I waited a short while, watching for the merest glint from any one of her many appendages. But she did, indeed, appear to be out cold. While it wasn't exactly a golden opportunity I was convinced that, with my stock at an all time low, one last cameo might pay dividends. So I quickly brewed up a pot of tea and coffee and slithered out from the safety of the curtain.

Keeping one eye firmly fixed on the rear of the cabin, I worked my way up the aisle. Some unpalatable expressions scrutinised my steps, as I tip-toed around the dirty crockery stacked up on the floor; barely-contained mutterings busily compared notes, lamenting my almost blasphemous disregard for symmetry and order. With this in mind, I stooped past them on the return leg to the galley and tried gathering up as many plates as possible.

At the front of the cabin, however, I was stopped by the tweedy gent's wife whose feet were protruding into the aisle. I waited in a sweltering daze as she struggled to loosen her shoes. I was almost about to reach down and help her, when suddenly she reared back and let out a shriek which momentarily drowned out the engine noise.

"A mouse!" she screamed, leaping to her feet. "There's a mouse! A mouse underneath my seat!"

She almost tore off my sleeve as I looked round at a pair of lizard eyes planted on the back row: the Blunderbuss menaced me with a glare that could have roasted a turkey. The rest of the aircraft, meanwhile, burst out into a carnival of acute hysteria. Breasted finials abdicated all domestic civility as they clung to their menfolk and the distress quickly spilt out into the aisle.

"Well do something you silly little man," came the echo from all sides.

I dropped down onto all fours, if only to escape a panic-ridden canopy now infested with horned mouths and warbling tongues. I scoured the cabin floor in the half-light, expecting to observe nothing more than a straying bun. But, as I worked my way through an increasingly abusive crowd, I finally caught sight of a tiny grey mouse racing toward the stowage locker. It had a terrific turn of speed and I could only watch as it disappeared down the ventilation grate running the length of the plane. The baying mob, however, were clamouring for blood, so I stood up smartly with my hands tightly cupped and declared:

"It's alright, ladies and gentlemen. I've caught the little blighter!"

Without waiting for a round of applause, I dashed into the WC to flush my 'prize' into the elements; but, with the lavatory clearly out of order, I simply opened the window a little. I then re-emerged into the cabin to face a collective frown that was now bound together by chapter and verse. It seemed to have spread like mascara as clouds of malignant energy burst in the clotted, stale air. Each pair of eyes pricked me repeatedly, puncturing a day that was already as flat as a pancake. Nobody said anything, they were all too busy listening to the Blunderbuss, who was feverishly broadcasting her thoughts through a bouffant of terrier-like hair. All I had to offer was a thousand apologies. But vibes were no longer furnished with hearts and minds and each gaze was padlocked in place. The situation was utterly beyond salvage and I squeezed up the aisle, knowing that any excuse, no matter how rotund, would now be lost on them all.

I retreated back to the cockpit and simply sat hoping to goodness that our little stowaway wouldn't re-appear. It struck me as a faintly biblical phenomenon; I couldn't fathom how a rodent might hitch a lift aboard a flying-boat cruising at 5000ft. I didn't dare look across at Ms Hammond in case she sniffed that something was amiss. But, with the passengers probably arguing about levels of compensation, I felt sure that a career barely twelve hours old, would soon be terminated.

15

There was thus little sense of relief when the lights of Valetta finally appeared. The white horses beckoned like sirens, curling their fingers as Miss Hammond let the plane down in uneven jerks. She seemed to dangle the aircraft on a rope that burned through her soft palms. A few feet from the surface, she gave out a final gasp and we splashed down with an undignified rumble.

She trotted the plane forwards as if working by candlelight, while I blindly rode tandem. The harbour front seemed completely still; just a few trawlers and tramp steamers were snoozing beneath a saw-tooth silhouette of roofs and steeples. Only a sprinkling of lights lingered like chippings in the narrow alleyways; they winked at us in a coarse, broken Morse as creatures staggered out into the night.

Approaching the quayside, Ms Hammond cut the engines and the nose swayed uneasily, until we bumped up against a small pier. A pair of young boys, uniformed by rags, threw down their fishing rods and quickly lassoed the bow. They gamely dragged the aircraft toward a mooring bollard and Ms Hammond pushed her head out through the side-screen.

"Thank you," she croaked, throwing them a couple of coins.

She then fell back into her seat with her complexion

yellowed by fatigue. It left me in no doubt that, for her, this was the end of the day. She had held back the boulder at her end, while I had a full-blown crisis to deal with. I got up slowly from my seat and prepared to face the wrath of our bottle-fed elders; I straightened out my cap and tunic and puffed myself up to a pyrrhic grandeur that must have resembled the Hindenburg.

Sweeping back the curtain, I half-expected to see our esteemed guests penned in their seats, holding up scorecards; but they were already standing by the door, clamouring to get out. They all looked the same to me now: androgynous beings wearing one hard scowl that had been beaten into place with a rolling pin. I prepared myself for their blows with a dignified glow and, of course, my regular old codger began first:

"Let me just say," the Blunderbuss barked, "that if I see you doing anything other than flying this plane, whilst we are airborne, then I shall demand to have it stopped. We can land wherever we happen to be; I'll walk the rest of the journey if need be. And, I can assure you, all these other passengers are of the same mind."

She wielded her crooked digit like a cut-throat razor and pointed along a line that was jostling to interrupt. I tried damming them all with genteel phrasing, devoid of exclamations. But, as I opened the door, their shop steward trotted out, towing plagiarized broadsides which had me rocking on my feet.

"This is quite the worst flight I have ever been on. We

have mice in the cabin, blocked toilets - whatever next for Heaven's sakes?"

Before I could draw breath, the next pair threw in their fireworks:

"I shall be demanding a full refund and an apology when I get back to England. The food and the service and the general standards of hospitality are more like something you'd find on a school trip."

Only Ms Hammond's brother-in-law offered any condolences, giving me a consolatory wink as he passed. The rest stepped outside trailing grievances that read like a wedding list. They marched in unison toward a waiting charabanc, emblazoned with the crest of the 'Royal Valetta Hotel'. As they huffed and puffed on board, I pitied the poor, unsuspecting concierge who was about to be overwhelmed by the stench of discontent. I could only guess how many, or how few, I'd see the following morning. But, in all honesty, it didn't really bother me - until I saw Ms Hammond standing at the end of the aisle.

"And what was all that about?" she said, fixing me to the spot with her blue eyes glinting like steel.

"Well," I stuttered, fumbling for words like a chef juggling pastries. "there were a couple of incidents during the flight."

"Like what exactly?"

"The toilet became blocked. But I can sort it out."

"Is that all?"

"There was also a slight problem with the dinner. I don't think it was a great success."

"So that's what all that commotion was about, was it? Blocked toilets and your lousy Ploughman's," she enquired, rapidly coming to the boil.

She stood poised to carve up whatever admission came next, so I just blurted it out regardless.

"One or two of the passengers also mistook me for the Captain, I'm afraid."

"So? So what?" she quipped.

"Well they – they felt that, perhaps, I wasn't spending enough time flying the plane."

"Why didn't you tell me about this earlier?"

"I didn't want to disturb you. Besides I simply said the plane was on automatic pilot."

"You bloody nit-wit. This plane doesn't have an autopilot."

"No, I realise that. But I'm sure none of the passengers will ever find out."

"Maybe not. But judging by what I just saw, they weren't exactly convinced by whatever you had to say."

Holding her voice like a hatchet in her hand, she stared at me with her red eyes bubbling, before thundering back up the aisle. She swept into the galley and, following in her wake, I watched from the edge of the doorframe as she poured herself a generous measure of gin. She then lapsed into silence, garnering an aura I didn't know how to read.

"It's bloody ridiculous isn't it?" she finally fanged out, facing the wall. "If flippin' Amy Johnson or bloody Beryl Markham so much as step into a plane they get splashed across the newspapers like film stars. But if someone like me just tries to make a living from flying then, of course, it's 'Oh no, we can't have that' and everyone's up in arms."

She probably had more to say but a fit of coughing butted in. It folded her over against the cupboards as she reached desperately for her handkerchief.

"You certainly made a bit of a mess when you were making the dinner, didn't you?" she spluttered, looking down at the Ploughman's mulch on the floor.

"Yes, I know. I'm sorry. I was just going to tidy up." I replied, pecking at some of the detritus with my fingers.

"Oh don't do it now. Leave it until the morning," she pleaded. "Is there anything left amongst all this lot? I'm absolutely famished."

I shuffled around her and began looking through the pile of cardboard boxes, now decorated with ground coffee and powdered milk.

"I don't think there's much room in here for the both of us," she said finally, sidestepping past me. "As I say, just stick some leftovers on a plate. I'm going out for a smoke."

I quickly assembled some edible sundries and then quietly ventured outside. I found Ms Hammond standing on the float, clinging to one of the struts like a plant on a trellis. She looked exhausted, to the point of helpless as she nurtured a slim cigarette. But she thanked me with a smile which flashed from her lips in a scarlet blink, like a lozenge rationed out on grease-proof paper. For a moment I watched as her downy shadow seemed to run off into the harbour and with it evaporated much of the din: the engine noise and irate caterwauling were no longer ringing in my ears.

"Would you like me to get you anything else?" I finally enquired.

"No, thank you. That was quite enough."

"What about your bag?" I said, hinting toward the stowage locker. "Would you like me to fetch it for you?"

"Why? What for?" she replied in a sombre voice.

"Well, I – I thought that perhaps we should think about turning in for the night."

Looking round slowly, she eyed me up and down while I stood floundering like a stray, lost in the rain; she tossed her cigarette out onto the water and stepped back inside the aircraft, before slumping into the nearest chair.

"Listen, I'm really sorry," she said biting her lip. "I meant to tell you all this earlier but I was in such a rush I just didn't get the chance. I'm afraid we're going to have to sleep on board. I'm sorry, I just don't have enough money. I should have explained the whole situation. I really do apologise. It's just that things have been so difficult lately. I simply had to go ahead with this flight - or else the receivers were going to come along and close the company down."

Wincing with discomfort, the stark details seemed to

pluck out her voice and another round of coughing set in. She dug into her pocket for a silver pill box, which she emptied out into her hand.

"I only took over a few months ago," she said, gulping down another admission. "I thought it was a dream come true until I saw the mountain of debt my father had accumulated. I had to sell our other two aircraft just to pay some bills. Of course, they were the best two we had and, to be honest, I'm not even sure if this old heap's entirely airworthy."

She stopped to light another cigarette and her eyes rolled up toward me with a laboured groan.

"The long and short of it is that this trip absolutely has to succeed otherwise it's curtains. But the big problem is that I haven't been able to contact all of our supply depots. I just hope they're all still operating. And I'm sorry if you thought this was going to be some lucrative little number because I won't be able to pay you very much. I hope Alec or my father explained that."

"Well, shall we just take each day as it comes?" I said, picking her plate up off the floor. "At least it'll be a good chance for me to see a bit of the world."

Her face brightened a little but the bouquet remained grey, as she trailed me into the galley. She shared another gin with the darkness peeping through the porthole, while the permed fumes from her cigarette curled their tails around her.

"So you'll just be hoping for the best," she murmured, "despite what I've told you."

"Yes, that's about it. There isn't much more we can do."

"You could go home."

"I wouldn't do that. I wouldn't desert you."

"Is that what they taught you in the RAF is it? Always go down with the ship?"

"No, that isn't what I meant at all." I insisted.

"Of course not, you're all given parachutes these days aren't you?" she said, letting out a feral laugh that caught me like a sting. "So you're an officer and a gentleman? Come to save a damsel in distress, is that it?"

"Well, no," I hesitated "at least, I'm certainly not an officer."

"Aren't you? I'm surprised with that plum in your voice. So how long have you been in the Air Force?"

"About a year."

"Is that all?" she sneered. "Good God, I knew I'd be scraping the bottom of the barrel but really. So how much flying experience do you have?"

"Well I've been in the Auxiliaries since University."

"Great. You must have logged at least a dozen hours. I must thank Alec when I next see him. And what did you do at university?"

"Classics."

"Classics! I thought you were going to say something useful like Engineering. A fat lot of good that's going to do us."

She shook her head in dismay, before glancing down into her glass like a spread of cards.

"All I remember from my Latin is that 'poenas' means 'punishment'," she sniggered. "But that's come in very handy, I must say."

She then referred back to the window and all my paltry utterances fluttered down around me, torn up like confetti. She took another thoughtful drag from her cigarette and the thickening smog began to obscure my view.

"Well - goodnight," I conceded reluctantly.

I desperately wanted to see her smile again and cursed myself for not sticking to my instructor's script. But, as I retreated back into the passenger cabin, I clung to the belief that tomorrow is always another day – providing we both got a good night's sleep.

16

Using a few seat cushions, I tried making myself comfortable on the floor; but there was more than just the echo of Ms Hammond's sentiments to keep me awake. At first, I ignored the faint scratching noise coming from somewhere beneath me; when the lights were snuffed out, however, I lay in the darkness thinking of nothing except suitcases being nibbled away in the hold.

Eventually, I hoisted myself up and wearily crept outside onto the float amid an excruciating air of farce. I quietly levered open the hatch and a playful twang scampered off into the night. It was too dark to see anything in the hold, so I clambered inside and started ploughing through tattooed luggage. But, as I dug down toward the bottom of the hull, some of the bags began to feel slightly damp; and, instead of any incriminating squeaks, I was sure I could hear water dripping.

The mouse hunt, nevertheless, continued until I had turned over the last of the suitcases. But the absurd situation suddenly darkened when I placed my hand down on an exposed section of the keel. It was completely submerged under three or four inches of water - and the level seemed to be rising up my sleeve. I quickly felt about for the source of the leak and found a small tear along a standing seam of rivets. A hot, stifling musk began to radiate around me like horse flies and I could think of nothing else except to hurriedly pile on some holdalls like sandbags. I kneeled down on top of them and waited alone in the darkness for a better idea to come along. But all I could hear was the harbour feeling its way around the plane, as if it were trying to find a way in.

With my trousers sopping, I sat almost embalmed by a haze of perspiration, until giant footsteps passed over my head. The beam from a flashlight then bounced off the bare metal walls of my cell and Ms Hammond appeared with her hair hanging down.

"What the hell are you doing in here?" she trumpeted gruffly, flashing her torch into my eyes. "I thought we were being burgled."

"I'm afraid we've got a bit of a problem - ."

"Oh Jesus," she interrupted, "you're like the bloody Archangel Gabriel aren't you? Always with the good news - so what is it now?"

"Well, we seem to be taking on water. It's not very much at the moment but there's some damage to the keel just here." I said, glancing down at my crudely-fashioned bung.

"Are you sure?" she said, bundling up her hair and leaning further inside. "What about the luggage, is everything OK?"

"Some of these bags are a bit wet. But we need to find some way to patch the hull tonight."

"Oh for goodness sake, can't it wait until the morning?"

I stared up at her through the gloom and took a moment before carefully rephrasing the situation.

"I'm afraid by the morning we'll probably find ourselves sitting in a submarine."

"What, you mean we're sinking? Christ Almighty!" she exclaimed. "What the hell are you going to do?"

"Is there any sort of repair kit on board?"

"No, no, not that I know of. Oh no, wait a moment," she said in a spin, " - at the back of the stowage locker there are some tools. Stay there, I'll go and fetch them."

She returned in an instant carrying a large toolbox; but it wasn't quite what I had in mind. Much of it was missing and the remains simply sat awaiting some everyday routine.

"There's nothing in here that's going to be much use." I said looking through a jumble of spanners. "Most of this stuff is for servicing the engines."

"Well why don't you have a think, for God's sake!" she shrieked as the aircraft began sporting a jaunty list.

"Do you know if any other flying-boat companies make a stop here?" I stuttered. "Maybe I could go and ask them for some help."

"No, no one else stops here. Besides, I'm not having that," she replied, with her silhouette quivering. "Absolutely not, you're not cosying up to anyone. Besides you should know how to fix it."

I had, of course, effected countless repairs to vehicles and machinery over the years but they were invariably made from iron or steel. I had only encountered aircraft-gauge aluminium when using the cooking utensils from my army-surplus camping kit. And if any of that ever needed repairing, I always turned to Renata. She had a special gift for caulking up burnt-through saucepans, using the worthless odds and ends she kept in a jar on the kitchen dresser. It didn't seem much to go on at first. But Ms Hammond's tactless remarks were starting to give me cramp.

"You know I did hire you on as a flight engineer," she goaded with increasing alarm. "You should have some idea as to what to do."

Somewhat generously, I failed to mention that it was probably her clumsy landing that had done the damage in the first place.

"If you can excuse me please, Ms Hammond. I'm just going to have a quick look in the galley. There might be something in there we can use."

Reluctantly she lifted her siege and I crawled out of the aircraft. But then I glanced back at the pile of hold-alls, quietly gestating like an unexploded bomb.

"You know, Ms Hammond, if you could climb inside and sit on top of all those bags," I said, carefully, "it might buy us some extra time."

She complied without a sound and I hobbled back inside the plane to see what I could scrounge. Unfortunately neither the galley nor the WC offered up any relevant parts; but, as I looked into the cockpit, the redundant navigator's chair looked perfect for our needs. I quickly set upon it with my penknife and ripped out all the hemp in the cushions. It also yielded a handful of large butterfly nuts which I stuffed into my pockets. I flew back down the aisle but Ms Hammond stopped me at the door - her face wrought by fury and fear.

"There's a bloody mouse in there! Did you know that?" she barked and hissed.

She was almost shaking with rage but I pushed past her and left her ablaze with a berserk refrain reverberating behind me:

"And what the hell have you done to this chair!?"

I clambered back inside the hold and began mixing up a mucky daub, using some grease I found in the toolkit and the innards from the navigator's chair. I then dug down through all the damp luggage, until the ghostly chill of the water seized my hand. Under the gaze of Ms Hammond's abandoned torchlight, I fumbled for the fracture along the keel and slapped down my water-proof mash. I worked it into the split with my fingers and, having removed the broken rivets, I hammered the seam closed. Some of the holes along the seam had suffered a little distortion but, mercifully, they were all still intact. I fed each one in turn with a cannibalised bolt before, quickly, tightening up the butterfly nuts.

"Well, have you fixed it?" Miss Hammond suddenly piped up from the hatch.

"I don't know yet," I replied, without looking round.

"Well surely we need to get rid of some of this water?"

She suggested impatiently. "Wait there, I'll see I can find a something."

She thumped back along the aisle and returned clutching a couple of ice buckets. For once we worked in quiet unison; relaying them back and fore we eventually emptied most of the water from the bottom of the hull.

"That's the best I can do." I said finally, falling back on my haunches.

"How's it looking now? Is it still leaking?"

"I can't tell for sure," I said slowly, watching for any further haemorrhaging. "But it seems to be holding."

"Well let's just hope for the best, shall we?" She said throwing her palm across her forehead "Come on, let's call it a day. I'm exhausted."

Somewhat to my surprise, she offered me her hand as I climbed out through the hatch; but then added a final proviso before I closed the door to the cabin.

"By the way," she asked abruptly, "did you get rid of that mouse?"

"No, I didn't see it; I suppose it must have drowned," I suggested.

"Well - we'd better have a look for it in the morning. I'm not too keen on mice and the last thing we want is for it to start wandering around the passenger cabin."

I didn't say anything else. Ms Hammond disappeared back behind the curtain and I settled down, as best I could, for the second time. Strangely, I didn't hear anymore more scratching. But as I laid my head on the floor, I said 'goodnight' to our little talisman and pushed a handful of crumbs through the ventilation grate in the aisle.

17

A conflict of perfumes aroused me the next morning, along with some monstrous belching. I looked up from the floor just as Ms Hammond was stepping out from the WC.

"Oh good, you're up. I was about to wake you," she snapped like a starting gun. "I've just unblocked the toilet, so there's no need for you to worry about that now. And I've put the bags that got wet out there on the pier to dry," she added, pointing out through the cardiganed windows. "Keep an eye on them; we don't any of them wandering off."

"What time is it?" I enquired.

"Five o'clock. We'll be departing in a couple of hours."

She stepped over me with her hosiery crunching joyously as she barrelled up the aisle.

"What about the hull?" I called out after her. "Did it let in any water during the night?"

"It looks alright to me. But you'd better check it yourself," she replied, before turning around. "I also need you to check both the engines and all the control surfaces. And make sure you get it all done before any of the passengers arrive. I don't want them to see you looking like some grease monkey. We definitely want to start off on the right foot with them today."

She disappeared into the galley, thick with braiding and epaulettes; it seemed that last night's news was now folded up and blotted with breakfast. It was still far too dark for me to do any maintenance on the engines, so I retired to the WC and prepared for another day of gunboat diplomacy and celluloid smiles.

Having re-crimped all my edges and seen off the worst of my stubble, I stepped outside to check on my repair. There was still a little water lying along the keel in the hold, but it didn't seem any worse than the night before. I was satisfied that it would withstand at least a couple more 'bumps' and I closed the hatch with a doting pride. But that wasn't quite enough for Ms Hammond's humourless authority and she emerged from the cabin, still riding high on ebullient cologne.

"By the way," she said, looking down at me from the pier. "Some of these suitcases are covered in your greasy finger marks. I tried shifting them with soapy water. But they're a devil to get off."

"A bit of petrol will have them out in no time," I assured her with a dwindling nod.

"Well, I don't have any petrol do I?"

"Perhaps that lot might be able to help," I replied, pointing toward a brace of fuel drums being marched along the pier.

"Oh it's Berto!" she cried out, spinning round.

She threw open her arms and skipped into the waiting embrace of a middle-aged figure, who bore a passing resemblance to Maurice Chevalier. Behind him were the two boys who had tied us up the night before, but now they were weighed down by re-fuelling apparel. I shelved my opinions with a gracious wave and looked on discreetly as they presented Ms Hammond with a swag of boxes and bottles. As if gliding on roller skates, she and her new friend disappeared inside the cabin, while the two boys set about refuelling the aircraft.

I was left like some sultry Danton, staring up at the port engine with a grease gun in my hand. Any indicators as to where the lubricating points might be, were long since lost beneath a viscous fury that all motors have in common. Nevertheless, I religiously scaled the side of the fuselage and began liberally squirting grease over the crankshaft casing and propeller bearings. I tried not to listen to the voices being carried joyously aloft from inside the aircraft. But, as I dragged myself over to the starboard side, I discreetly peered down through the cockpit canopy. Ms Hammond was standing on the flight deck fixed to a rather precious gait, while her friend beseeched her in small steps. Perhaps there was a perfect explanation for their close-quarter smiles and the saloon-and-barber whispers; but my view was distorted by a pebble vision that saw only his cavalier laugh brandishing fortified teeth.

I eventually put away my galleried gawp and continued working my way around the cylinder heads. When all the carburettors were weeping greasy smears, I leaned back like a monkey against one of the struts; I looked out across the harbour at the congregation of shapes that had left me guessing the night before: casement windows now reached across narrow lanes trying to steal a kiss, while Byzantine corbels kneeled up in prayer against medieval walls. Such innocuous devotion was easily drowned out by the vernacular bellows, which blew like a chilly wind among black-laced figurines.

Our precious schedule seemed to fall by the wayside, until Ms Hammond and her friend finally re-emerged from the aircraft. She embraced him once again but he continued to bend her ear, while the two boys tossed the luggage back inside the hold.

"Thank you so much once again Berto," she called out with a big wave as he wandered away, leaving his urchins tidying up the pier.

I tried to slip unnoticed back into the cabin but Ms Hammond came whistling down the aisle behind me.

"Oh Berto's such a sweetie. Look at all this!" she said, ushering me into the galley. "We've got enough plonk now to last for the rest of the trip - and these smell absolutely wonderful."

"What are they?" I asked, as she stood savouring a line curious-looking pies.

"I'm not sure exactly what he called them. He said his mother makes them. They look like quiches or flans, don't they? But I'm sure they'll go wonderfully with all the green salad we've got left over. Now, come on," she added, glancing at her watch. "if I'm going to be looking after the passengers on this next leg. I must go through the charts with you."

She led me back onto the flight deck and, having pulled out a map, she swept her hand across the top of a continent still unburdened by any real borders.

"Right, Do you know the eastern Med at all?" she said, reverting back to her gilded tongue

"No I'm afraid not."

"Well, it's quite straightforward getting from here to Port Said, the safest bet is to fly on a bit of a dogleg - then you can simply follow the coastline up to Alexandria. But don't get too close until you're into Egypt; the Italians can be a bit anti-social these days."

She quickly pointed out place names that plundered the alphabet, just as the first of the passengers began returning to the plane.

"Oh Chr-umbs," she mumbled, peering past the door. "OK. I'll look after all the meeting and greeting. You stay here and study that and don't show your face whatever you do."

Drawing the curtain firmly behind her, she cantered up the aisle and began her front-of-house courtship. Our cargo of underwired buffoons offered her only a passing glance as they marched on board - with most resolutely refusing any assistance. Fierce armorials carefully arranged their crotch before taking to their seats; and their frothy topped companions strangled their calves and contorted their pelvis as they paraded yet another new outfit.

When Ms Hammond announced our impending

destination they were not remotely dazzled - nor were they tickled by the mention of pith helmets and Bermuda shorts. Like a flower in a farmyard, she was soon mired in fuss and frayed nerves as an outbreak of Goldilocks syndrome took hold. Ladies began to nag while the men geed them on like kites. But, working her way slowly down the aisle, she patiently ladled out irresolute promises before shoring them all up with gobstoppers, newspapers and a few pompous cushions. Even the Blunderbuss eventually buttoned her bulldog clip and she nestled among the fag heads on the back row who sat sucking in her thoughts. Amazingly, our payload was complete – except for Ms Hammond's brother-in-law. But even he eventually staggered back into the aircraft, looking as though he'd spent the night in a ditch.

"Sorry about that everyone. Ruddy casino staff forgot to wake me," he said apologising to the rest of the cabin. "It's all written here, they can't even read." He laughed, pointing to his flight ticket which he'd pinned to his lapel.

Ms Hammond strained with a smile, before closing the cockpit door.

"Bloody bastard Boer trekker, good mind to leave without him," she muttered, as she climbed into her seat. "Right, I'll get us in and out, there are a few sand bars and reefs which can sometimes move about a bit, and we need to watch out for crocodiles when we're coming in to land at Port Said."

"I can't say I've encountered crocodiles before," I said,

trying to embellish my pedigree.

"I'll bet you haven't," Miss Hammond said softly. "But I lost one of our 'boats at Port Said last year and I really don't want it to happen again. They're usually only a problem in the winter months when there's a flare path – the bright lights seem to draw them in. A couple of low passes gets rid of them; only wished to God that would work on the rest of the wildlife."

Her voice petered out as each engine stretched on its ends and I watched the needles stuttering like fiddles. There was the usual gasping whine and slap of pistons as each propeller was whipped to a bud. It was a prelude I never tired of hearing. But sadly radial science is, now, almost completely extinct. It is still practised but only by fanatics burdened by loathsome wives.

18

With the aircraft pulsating like an artery, we stumbled off the water and continued our nomadic yomp. Excitable outbursts followed us to the edge of the headland and our departure was probably preserved in commemorative scrimshaw. Ms Hammond stared into the elements like some old salt, before trimming the aircraft and planting us on a course.

As I awaited my turn at the wheel, I sat scrutinising every inch of her repertoire but was soon contending with a tearful squint. The sun began bearing down through the canopy glass and perspiration trickled out from under my cap. The heat pulled on my collar and any bare metal parts quickly become too hot to touch. It didn't seem to matter to her, however, she simply carried on, tweaking any deviation from her course.

While she flew, that was everything: the sentence for smashing her tea-sets and refusing to wear jodhpurs. She chased the horizon through an immaculate blue wilderness, far removed from any balance sheets splashed with red ink. I watched her as if waiting for a dance but she seemed loathe to give up her repetitive strains. With my eyes half-closed, I simply sat dripping with each passing minute and started sneezing at regular intervals until, finally, she checked me against her watch.

"OK. Your turn," she called out, slowly standing up. "Keep a bead on the compass heading at all times and we should reach the coast of North Africa in about an hour or so."

I gripped the column like a spaniel as the heat bit into my hands and Ms Hammond watched me from the back of the cockpit, before finally pulling the door closed.

At first, the nose nodded sneeringly, seemingly reluctant to accept a new hand at the helm and there was a constant negotiation, conducted via a long chain of command. Compared to the Moth, all the controls felt stiff; but with each adjustment, I slowly began to get a feel for the aircraft and its character: that unquantifiable which afflicted almost all machines before the days of oriental fanaticism.

Behind me I could hear the chinking of glasses and the occasional scent wafted through: pedigree nicotine and well-bred alcohol spun off from bloated corpuscles. Perhaps they would be pleased to see her as she entered, bearing fabulous canapés and choreographed semantics, which I had failed to master. But there was also a good chance that all her efforts might be undone by baited insinuations - amplified by the necessity to shout. The women would most probably be sitting crippled by flushes and turns, ready to condemn her as just a silly thing needing a shot of plaisir d'amour. Men called Rex, meanwhile, would doubtless be reaching out like napkinned octopus, having branded her as a possible mistress. In the face of such antagonism, I could only hope that Ms Hammond was conducting herself as if she were more than a gentleman – or, failing that, simply plugging her mouth with her fist.

Fortunately, when she re-appeared at my side, there was no seismic entrance - just a touch of damson staining her cheeks. She bent over the back of her chair and looked across the swathe of instruments, which I was doing my best to ignore. I expected her to immediately re-assume command but she simply stood with her hands clasped together, as if embalmed by the heat. We both stared into the distance, until the sea began to lose its composure and an auburn crumble rose up through a musk-like haze.

As the threshold of North Africa came into view, I pushed the column over to port and the aircraft responded like a range being hauled. When the wings finally began to bank, there was a muffled cacophony behind us, which seemed to spell out 'crockery' in onomatopoeia.

"Take it easy, for goodness sake. You're not flying a fighter in the RAF now," Ms Hammond yelled, as if I'd forgotten my ear trumpet. "I'd better go and serve the lunch - before it serves itself."

She left me staring at a cruel coastline that hissed at the water's edge; countless dry shades seemed to lie prostrate for miles. Africa had always been described to me as a cornerstone of Empire; a playground for seventh son bounders who were determined not to live each day as they would the next. But all I saw was a depleted landscape, donated by some godless planet. It all looked utterly alien – but, perhaps, no more so than some other places which I was supposed to have called my own; every time I visited London I was usually left dumbstruck by a populace that still seemed to adhere to the rudiments of natural selection: instead of the quiet, eternal routines which I was used to, there were eruptions outside the pubs at nightfall; and it had been no surprise to learn that Ms Hammond had once thrived in the midst of 'the smoke'. I could just imagine her darting like a cab driver through the rain-coated traffic, back to some Bloomsbury mews where a half-hearted liaison probably lingered like the washing-up. What was odd was why she had chucked it all in, only to incarcerate herself amongst all the things she seemed to despise most.

The steady drool of the engines was, in itself, enough to test anyone's sanity. But it remained remarkably quiet in the passenger cabin behind me; I didn't even hear Ms Hammond stepping back into the cockpit.

"Do you want anything to eat?" she said suddenly, placing her hand on my shoulder. "I'm just going to tidy everything away. But I'll bring you a snack if you want it."

"No, I'm fine thank you very much."

"What about a drink?"

"No, thanks," I said, looking round. "Is everything alright back there with you?"

"It's OK. A lot of them have fallen asleep now. Thank God."

Her voice had none of the bark that I was used to hearing and, for a while, she seemed reluctant to leave the sanctuary of the cockpit; she simply crouched down next to me as if trying to catch her breath. When I glanced across again, she smiled stoically but an ashen cloud scoured her face to a veinless marble. For the first time, it didn't take a jeweller's scrutiny to see the strain of navigating between polarised opinions.

Eventually, she returned to dispense more social graces and etiquette, leaving me alone with just an annoying crosswind for company. For a moment, a rainbow appeared; but it was quickly swallowed up by the bizarre abstractions that occasionally burst out, as if the scrubland was venting its thoughts. They contorted the coastline in granite spasms which seemed to melt away beneath the sun's derision, leaving just a weepy trail of spoil and rubble.

There was little else to punctuate our lazy lurch, except a few up-turned fishing boats. Only the Italian block houses appeared at regular intervals to measure our progress. They stood guarding road junctions which were nothing more than faint crosses scratched in the sand. But they didn't look to be garrisoned; in fact the whole landscape was remarkably lifeless. Even when a town or village emerged from the dirt, children sometimes waved but they were usually ushered indoors. The people seemed reluctant to bend their gaze and, invariably, we left behind just brave mules standing in the heat. It was as if the shout of the cylinders threatened them with fire and brimstone - or the words bruising our flanks promised a curse upon anyone who read them.

At least there was some relief from the heat as dusk began plucking the sun's fury; although the drop in temperature left my seat feeling more like a teabag. The slightest movement became unpleasant and so I coagulated at the helm, until an apron of verdigri heralded the arrival of the Nile Delta.

It was an almost convalescing sight, after so many hours languishing in a world where things were stored and eaten alive: diamond-cut waterways began threading through a cultivated sea where arrow-headed flocks kindly signposted the way. Sloops drifted like lanterns with their buxom sails glowing white in the sunset. They illuminated our path to Alexandria, where awning-covered streets danced to the applause of twinkling mosques. People were greeting one another like butterflies in lavish robes that rippled in the breeze - and shirtless fishermen waved at us joyously, as if hoping to catch a ride. They urged us on, flattering our progress and all too quickly we left them behind. Our weary wings seemed to sag a little; but the lofty palm groves continued on with us for miles afterwards, ready to donate their feathery leaves.

The unfurling spectacle fulfilled all my notions of Egypt and I expected Port Said to emerge before us, bathed in the shimmering sunset. But as the marshes and wetlands began to peter out, a thickening slick of tankers appeared from beyond the horizon. They were all worming their way toward an arsenal of funnels girdled by a lagoon-shaped harbour, where burly tug boats were doing their best to keep some sort of order.

With the light fading fast and our fuel dwindling, I immediately throttled back and started working through as many of Ms Hammond's checks as I could remember. Crocodiles, however, looked to be the least of my worries because, as I circled slowly overhead, I could see hardly any space for us to set down. Port Said was just a patchwork of floating silos penned in by a wintry layer of concrete. It certainly wasn't an ideal spot to attempt my first ever landing in a flying-boat – so, once again, I shelved any sense of gallantry and waited patiently for Ms Hammond's return.

When she finally thumped back into her seat, she looked lighter by several pounds of flesh but immediately took over at the controls. She pushed the column forwards and we dropped down low over the harbour, coming within inches of some of the ships' masts and antennas. At first, I couldn't understand what she was doing; she just sat grim faced as we sped past startled sailors who were hanging out their washing. She then pulled up sharply over the town and, promptly, repeated the manoeuvre. This time, however, the tug boats began scurrying about below us, shepherding vessels out of the way. Remarkably, within a few minutes, they had cleared a stretch of the harbour and Ms Hammond finally brought us into land. We settled into the water some distance from the quayside where, to my surprise, she then switched off both the engines.

"Christ I'm absolutely exhausted," she groaned, before resting her head on the control column.

"Well if you tell me which way to go, I'll dock the aircraft if you like," I suggested.

"No. No. We have to wait here until customs has checked us out. If they're not here in a couple of minutes, though, we'll have to deploy the drogues."

I wasn't too sure what 'the drogues' were exactly but was rather more concerned by the proximity of all the other vessels around us. As they criss-crossed the harbour, the aircraft began pitching heavily and I craned my neck through the side screen to see none of them were getting too close. Ms Hammond, however, didn't seem to be the least bit bothered and just sat with her eyes shut - until there was a thump against the fuselage.

"Oh God. Brace yourself," she mumbled beneath a belch. "Here comes the Port Said welcoming committee."

We both peered over the bow and watched as a group of bedraggled children clambered out of a canoe. Within moments, they were up onto the nose and pressing their faces against the canopy glass. I immediately yelled at them through the window, in an oafish baritone which I barely recognised.

"Don't waste your breath," Ms Hammond sighed coolly. "I'll just give them some of these – usually gets rid of them," she said, pulling a packet of cigarettes out of her pocket.

Like some deranged Santa, she then began handing

them out as if they were sweets. But it made little difference; the pint-sized pirates simply snapped them all up, before moving further along the fuselage.

"Bloody urchins," Ms Hammond spat, as they started swinging from the struts and dangling trinkets in front of the cabin windows. "They're sodding everywhere this time. Quick. Go and stand by the cabin door. Make sure none of them get in," she said biting her lip. "I'll fire up the engines – hopefully that'll scare them off."

With the propellers now resembling a climbing frame, that didn't strike me as a very sound idea. In fact, it seemed sure to end in disaster and, for the first time, I felt compelled to object. But, fortunately, a loud hoot from a klaxon interrupted her, just as she was beginning the starting procedure.

"Oh thank God for that," she sighed as a motor launch christened 'Douane' finally appeared.

The swarm of youngsters adorning the aircraft suddenly dived like dolphins into the water and were away in their canoe.

"This lot will tow us to our mooring," she said quietly, as the launch drew up alongside. "But, here, he'll want to see this."

She handed me a burnished wallet, which I duly passed to a po-faced official who popped up by my window.

"Your flag?" he immediately snapped.

"Oh hell, I forgot about that." Ms Hammond

exclaimed.

She hastily fished out a small blue ensign from under her seat and pushed it up through a hole in the canopy. The customs officer peered in and looked at her with an almost pained expression, before glancing back toward me. I gave him a polite, dum dum smile which seemed enough to explain the unorthodox hierarchy on board; but it left his pencil moustache twitching uncomfortably and he quickly lost interest in any paperwork.

Having returned Ms Hammond's wallet, he instructed his crew to hitch a rope up to our bow; the aircraft creaked uncomfortably and we were dragged toward an extremity of Port Said where another throng were waiting, primed by the scent of finery. They watched us with egg-box grins, dressed in dusters and dishcloths, ready to haggle to infinity; but, fortunately, they were held in check by a brigade of bell boys from the local hotel. That seemed to be of little consolation to Ms Hammond, however, who buried her face in her hands as we bumped up against the pier.

"Oh God, here we go again," she groaned. "Can you see to the passengers, please. I've had a belly full from them already today."

I was happy to oblige as I desperately needed to stretch my legs and get a breath of fresh air. I assumed our payload of corsets and collar studs would be equally keen to be released; but upon entering the passenger cabin, I found most of them dozing amid a thick haze of alcohol.

I crept down the aisle and began rousing them gently but was almost upended by empty wine bottles, which rolled out from underneath the seats. Eventually, they rose like doughy lumps and I coaxed them outside with cheery mutterings about goat's milk baths and other decadent treatments. They all looked badly creased after such a long stretch in the cabin; all except for the Blunderbuss, who emerged from the toilet looking as though she'd spent the day in curlers.

"You're going to have to fetch me my luggage from the hold, if you don't mind," she demanded. "I can't keep going around wearing the same suit day after day."

Unusually for her, it was a rather subdued protest with the words being almost mouthed, as if she didn't want the other passengers to hear. I couldn't help but suspect that she was bristling at the sight of a faux pas by her peers. If that was the case, however, her travelling companion no longer cut much of an accomplice: in fact, as he stood swaying next to her with his trousers hitched up around his naval, he looked more like W.C. Fields.

"I'll be waiting in the car. And remember it's the small shagreen trunk I want," she scowled, before nudging him in the ribs. "Have you got that?"

He gave her a vacant nod and we both watched her trundle away down the gangplank toward a waiting convoy of taxis.

"I don't know why she wants it," he sighed. "The

chances are she won't be able to find the key – and then I'll probably get the blame. Oh goodness," he then remarked forlornly, as I opened up the hold. "It's too dark in there to see anything. If you like I can just say we couldn't find it. I don't want to be a bother. I can come back in the morning when there's more light."

"No, no, it's quite alright." I assured him. "I'll find it. But, just tell me again, what am I looking for?"

"It's a pea-green box covered in shark skin," he said, before succumbing to a snorting giggle. "Probably some relative of hers, I shouldn't imagine."

As I clambered inside, a variety of hides all seemed to groan in the darkness like a cadence of latent bellows; but, of course, I had to empty out half the hold before, finally, unearthing the small, green trunk in question.

"That's it! That's the one," the Blunderbuss's companion cried – and one of the bell boys immediately rushed up and carried it away. "Thank you so much, my good man. Here you are. This is for all your trouble. Have a drink on me," he added, handing me half a crown. "In fact, I tell you what, have another one. Go and buy that lovely filly in there a drink, as well," he said, peering in through the cabin door. "Lovely ankles on that one. I'd keep my eye on her, if I was you."

He gave me a stern slap on the back and some more words of encouragement from the end of the pier.

"Good night - and good hunting," he called out, with

his hand in the air.

I waved back but I didn't feel entirely comfortable with that second half crown in my hand. I had never seriously entertained the idea of stepping beyond my remit: Ms Hammond was high up on a pedestal and, now that I knew her a little better, I was quite happy with that arrangement. Besides, Port Said was hardly the place to start my courting career; and, as if to vindicate my conduct, Ms Hammond then banged on one of the cabin windows and frowned at me through the glass.

"What are you doing? Why are all these bags out here?" she demanded, as she stepped out onto the float.

"One of the passengers wanted their luggage."

"Well don't leave anything lying around, otherwise those thieving buggers will have it," she said, glancing at a blizzard of rags still hanging about by the harbour wall. "We need to make damned sure we lock the hatch securely tonight. So here, you'll need this."

She handed me a small key and I slowly began returning all the luggage to the hold. Ms Hammond looked on pensively for a while, scolding her systems with yet another cigarette until a couple of suitcases caught her eye.

"Aren't those the two bags that should have been picked up at Marseilles?" She asked, looking down at the labels. "Yes, that's right, 'Beauchamp'. I tell you what, leave those - I'll take them inside."

Somewhat hurriedly, she lugged both suitcases into the

cabin, where she immediately began disembowelling one of them. I peered in like a frail butler and watched as fine garments and eveningwear started flying through the air. By the time I had locked the hold, garish colours had been strewn across the seats like silken graffiti.

"Here, catch," she said chucking me a packet of playing cards, the moment I stepped into the cabin. "We can hand these out on the next leg. Hopefully it'll keep some of the passengers quiet - I can only dish out so much booze. Not much else in that one, though," she added, pushing the first suitcase to one side.

"Were you looking for something in particular?"

"Yes, salvage," she muttered as she attempted to open the second suitcase. "Here give me a hand with this one – it seems to be locked."

"Are you not going to return them to their owners then?"

"Don't you know what salvage is?" she replied sharply. "It means finders keepers. Anyway, they don't want any of this stuff – and my needs are greater. Come on, don't just stand there. Help me get it open."

I tugged on the lid a couple of times but it was a pointless endeavour. Both suitcases were the finest that Bond Street's engineers had to offer and, besides, I was somewhat reluctant to get involved.

"Come on!" Ms Hammond shouted. "Give it a good pull."

"But I don't want to damage it."

"That, my dear, is the whole point of the exercise. Now, come on, have another go."

"It's not going to work, Ms Hammond. These are really good solid locks. Do you want me to see if there's something in the toolbox we can use."

"No, no," she grumbled. "Let's try again in the morning. Although, maybe the end of my nail file would work," she said, crouching down and scrutinising the escutcheons. "Oh, let's forget it for now. I suppose we both need our beauty sleep."

She thumped the top of the suitcase and left me alone in the cabin, feeling small enough to fit into her pocket. I was inclined to take both suitcases straight back to the hold, hoping that by the morning she'd have forgotten about them. But I had a sudden change of heart when she re-emerged from behind the curtain with a very large pistol in her hand.

"Do you know what this is?" she demanded.

"Well, it looks like a - "

"It's a flare gun," she interrupted. "There's no lock on the cabin door, so if anyone tries to get in, just point this at them. But be careful it's loaded."

As she handed it to me by the barrel, I found myself swallowing hard but I gamely tried to see it as yet another promotion – this time, from pilot to guard dog.

19

All night long, the aircraft seemed to sway uneasily as shouts and howls were kicked around the harbour. More than once, I awoke with a jolt, convinced that someone was turning the door handle. I grasped the flare gun ready to charge outside yelling blue murder. But, invariably, the sound turned out to be Ms Hammond's footsteps as she paced around the flight deck, smothering another cough.

I found it difficult to believe that her finances were so dire, as to warrant stealing from the passengers. But, at first light, I awoke to see her, once again, standing over the suitcase which had defeated us both the night before.

"Done it!" she said, popping the catches. "Right let's see what we have in here."

She threw open the lid and pulled out a couple of ball gowns which she held under her chin.

"So, how much do you think we can get for these?" she asked sharply, as I propped myself up on the floor.

"I really couldn't tell you." I replied.

"Well, this morning, you're going to find out. Mind you, some of these are absolutely beautiful. I'm tempted to keep one or two for myself," she said, running a silk scarf through her fingers.

"Ms Hammond," I said as I slowly staggered to my feet. "surely those are still someone else's property -

regardless of whether or not they've been left behind."

"Maybe. Maybe you're right. But quite frankly I'm past questioning what is right - and proper. As I have explained to you already, I'm running this operation on a rather tight budget - in fact," she said pulling a bundle of pound notes from her jacket, "this is all the money I've got left. Most of my suppliers seem to have vanished and this is probably only going to cover our fuel costs. It almost certainly isn't enough to get us re-stocked with provisions; that's where all this lot is going to come in handy," she said, referring back to the suitcases.

"So you're seriously proposing to sell all that lot?"

"Why not? No one else seems to want them and everything's got a price in this blinkin' cess pit."

"But, Ms Hammond, we're not even halfway to Darwin. What are you going to do at the next stop and the one after that and the one after - ."

"I've got it all covered, thank you very much."

"I suppose next you'll be selling bits of the plane as souvenirs," I mumbled under my breath.

"Damn it! If you don't think it's such a brilliant idea then why don't you see how far this lot gets you," she yelled, thumping the money into my chest.

She threw open the cabin door and, almost immediately, a gaggle of hawkers came scampering along the pier.

"And if by some miracle you succeed - you'll earn my

undying admiration," she added scornfully, before producing a page torn from the Pilot's Notes. "This is how much petrol we need and the correct octane. So - off you go."

"Wouldn't it be safer for me to have a couple of cheques instead?" I suggested limply, glancing down at the wad of notes in my hand.

"How many times do I have to tell you? That's all the money I've got left. So what you're going to do is button that lot up inside your tunic - because if you lose it, we're stuck here. Now get going."

She slammed the door behind me as soon as I had stepped outside and I paraded along the gang-plank, almost tripping on my shoe-laces. I pushed past the waiting congregation with a perpetual apology; but when I stopped on the quayside to get my bearings, my pale sounds were quickly overwhelmed by an unsavoury miasma. Concubations pounced with withering advances which seemed to burrow into every orifice. Spidery hands and barnacled fingers tugged on my sleeves and admired my cufflinks. I tried asking for directions and, at first, all I got was laughter and squabble. Eventually, however, I was lured toward a heaving bazaar where stalls lingered in twilight.

With Ms Hammond's money poking me in the ribs, I pigeon-stepped through belligerent barter; my nappy skin was greeted with plants, furniture, rugs and kittens - which looked almost good enough to eat. Caged creatures were dangled in front of me, while to my left and right, jars were scooped out and savoured by pimpled probosces. But there was nothing that looked remotely suitable for our discerning clientele; nor did anyone seem to have the slightest idea as to where I might be able to find any petrol.

Amid the asphyxiating muesli, my resolve quickly began to wilt and I was sorely tempted to give up, when I spotted a uniform in the crowd not too dissimilar to mine.

"Excuse me," I shouted, desperately grabbing at a burly Merchant mariner.

"Hey, steady on," he said, swinging round. "I was hoping to keep both arms on this jacket."

"I'm so sorry. But you wouldn't know where I might be able to get hold of some petrol, would you?"

"Well," he said smiling through the din, "you can get almost anything in this place. Surely it's fuel oil you want, though?" he asked, before glancing at my cap badge. "Oh, I see, you're a birdman. I saw that flying-boat sitting in the staging pen. Are you the skipper?"

"Yes - for my sins," I replied.

"*Peninsular & Orient* are probably your best bet. That's where we get most of our supplies. I'm just heading that way myself, if you want to tag along."

"Glad to. Thanks very much."

With just the right amount of haughty, he scythed through the snake-oil sermons, until we finally re-emerged outside.

"The name's Turnbull, by the way, *Empress of Siam*,"

he said, stroking the braid on his cap. "Is this your first time in Port Said?"

"Yes," I nodded, half-heartedly returning his salute.

"I thought so," he went on, looking across at my lapel. "Can't say I've ever heard of 'Imperial Air Services'. Is that the same outfit as Imperial Airways?"

"No, no, we're just a small, private operation," I replied.

"So, how far are you heading?"

"To Darwin - Australia."

"That's quite a hike. I'd offer to give you a tow but I'm only going as far as Rangoon," he grinned. "As I say, I can't guarantee *P&O* will be able to help but they should, at least, be able to put you in touch with someone who can. They're usually pretty good though; in fact, me and my lads use them like a bloomin' NAAFI a lot of the time. These are their offices just up here on the right."

Choking on the smell of tyred and hoofed transport, we finally reached a gated gateaux; it sat prim and proud and wanting for nothing as the menagerie of vehicles crawled past. An army of gardeners were dusting the shrubs and, as soon as we were inside, a page boy rushed up desperate to assist us.

"Do you fancy some breakfast?" Captain Turnbull asked me. "They have a nice buffet over there by the bar, its only 5 bob."

He pointed out toward a courtyard at the rear where drinks were being served. I was desperately hungry and couldn't help but watch for a moment as itinerant Empire fodder waltzed around the colonnades, before reclining upon foie gras furniture.

"No, no. I really ought to get on. I'm running to rather a tight schedule." I finally replied.

"Suit yourself," Captain Turnbull shrugged. "It's the top floor you want - a chap called Huggins. Don't let the name fool you, though, he can be a grumpy old goat. But just tell him I sent you and he should brighten up a little. And if you don't get an answer at his door, just go straight in. He's usually on his balcony watering his plants."

"Well, thank you so much for all your help, Captain Turnbull," I said shaking his hand. "I really don't know what I would have done without you."

"That's quite alright. Best of luck - and if you change your mind afterwards, I'll buy you an iced tea. It's the best way to cool down around here," he smiled. "You look as if you could do with one."

"Thanks. I'll bear it in mind."

Captain Turnbull was then led away by the page boy and I dragged myself up the stairs to the top floor. Sure enough, there was no reply when I reached the office of 'J. Huggins – Quartermaster', so I peered inside. A short, tubby figure was standing on a terrace surrounded by flora and, as I stepped up to his desk, he turned and glared at me.

"Isn't it customary to knock before entering?" he asked gruffly as he came in off his balcony.

"I'm sorry, I did. But you obviously didn't hear me." I replied.

"Well, what is it you want?" he asked, squinting at me through a pair of pebble glasses an astronomer might have made.

"I was hoping you might be able to help me. I desperately need to get hold of some fuel."

"Oh for goodness sake, this is ridiculous. Who are you and where are you from?" he asked angrily, straining to look at my uniform.

"I came on the recommendation of Captain Turnbull." I said slowly removing my cap.

"Turnbull? Never heard of him," Huggins snapped back.

"He's the skipper of the *Empress of Siam*. He said you might be able to help."

"Young man, I look after the needs of over 300 vessels all flying the P&O flag. And half the time it seems I'm expected to re-supply ships from almost every other fleet entering this wretched place. I'm sorry but I just don't have time to be playing the Good Samaritan to every Tom, Dick and Harry who waltzes in through my door. You'll just have to try one of the other shipping companies."

"Well - is there someone you could recommend?" I said, feeling rather deflated.

"No, there is not. Now if you don't mind I'm very busy," he said tucking himself in at his knee-hole.

"The situation is rather desperate. Can't you at least point me in the right direction?"

"No, I can not," Huggins said without looking up. "Now good day to you."

There was then a knock on the door and young clerk marched straight in with a large book wedged under his arm.

"Oh, I'm so sorry sir," he said, stopping in his tracks as soon as he saw me. "I didn't know you were with someone."

"That's quite alright Cathcart. Come on in. This gentlemen was just leaving," Huggins replied, glancing toward me. "So how did you get on? Did you manage to find someone?"

"Well, unfortunately, sir, there doesn't seem to be anyone available presently," the clerk replied.

"But what about the kitchen staff? Have you been down there?"

"Yes, sir, and I was informed that both the French chefs won't be in until sometime this afternoon."

"What?" Huggins gasped. "But what about breakfast? Who prepares that?"

"I did ask about that, sir, and I was informed that the French chefs don't cook English Breakfast."

"Oh for goodness sake," Huggins exclaimed. "But we've got to get this to the printers by this afternoon."

"Well, sir, if it's any help, I took the precaution of borrowing this from the reading room," the clerk said, holding up a French dictionary in his hand. "My French at school wasn't too bad, if you want me to have a go."

"No, I'm sorry Cathcart, we can't risk any mistakes." Huggins replied, before letting out a piercing shriek just as I was walking out the door. "Hey, you there. Just a minute. You can't speak French, can you?"

"Possibly. But if you remember rightly I was just leaving," I muttered from the threshold.

"Listen. Can you or can't you?" Huggins demanded in a sweat.

"Well, it all depends," I replied, shuffling slowly back into the room, "because, you see, at the moment I'm rather tied up - trying to source some supplies."

"If you can translate this for me by lunchtime today I'll get you any supplies you need," he said, handing me an 'Order of Ceremony' for a banquet scheduled for that weekend.

"Looks quite straight forward," I said, giving it a cursory glance.

"But it has to be absolutely word perfect," Huggins insisted. "Because it's for a dinner to mark the anniversary of the building of the Canal. There's going to be a number of French dignitaries there, so there can't be any mistakes or cock-ups, do you understand? Otherwise the Foreign Office are going to come down on me like a ton of bricks."

"As I say, I could do it for you."

"Are you absolutely sure?"

"My proficiency is better than average - if that's good

enough," I said looking him in the eye. "My nanny was from Alsace."

"Alright then," Huggins said, pointing to the other side of his desk, "take a seat there and, whilst you're doing that, I'll sort out whatever supplies you need. Agreed?"

"Seems fair."

"Thank you, Cathcart, that'll be all," he said, despatching his secretary, who looked a little put out. "So, what is it you need altogether?" Huggins then asked, as I pulled up a chair.

"I need fuel - and some provisions for the passengers."

"OK, and how large is this vessel of yours?"

"Well, actually, it's a flying-boat."

"A flying-boat? Oh, you're with Imperial." He said squinting at my badge. "But I thought Imperial stopped at Alexandria, not Port Said."

"They've obviously changed their itinerary. I haven't been with the company very long."

"Flying-boats aren't really my area of expertise. But I'm sure I can sort something out. How many souls on board?"

"Sixteen plus the crew," I replied.

"And what do you require as regards fuel?"

"450 gallons - 95 octane."

"Right. Sounds like high-grade stuff," he said making some notes. "I'd probably have to order that in specially. When do you need it by?"

"Some time this morning." I replied.

"Oh crikey. Well, the only petrol I have here is for the transport pool. You know, trucks and that sort of thing. Will that do?"

"No, it has to be proper aviation fuel."

"Well, maybe I can get it - but not by this morning."

"Then, in that case," I said slowly slipping my pen back into my pocket. "perhaps you'll need to find someone else to translate this little lot."

"OK, OK. Hold your horses," Huggins snapped back in a fluster. "I'll get straight onto 'Supplies' and see what they can do. What about a drink, by the way, do you want something cold? My secretary can fix up anything you want. Juice? Tea? Gin? Scotch?"

"No, I'm fine thank you very much." I replied.

"Right, well, let me know if you change your mind," he stuttered. "But just excuse me for a moment, would you? I need to make a couple of 'phone calls."

While I set about translating his paperwork, Huggins began bawling at some far away exchange. Unfortunately this was a land where operators had yet to be bred in captivity and he rocked uncomfortably back and fore like a jockey, as he waited to be put through.

"So, your suppliers have left you high and dry have they?" he asked, with his hand over the receiver.

"Something like that." I replied, without looking up.

"Bloody cowboys. They're everywhere in this miserable place. I've been here almost 5 years now and I still haven't got used it. If it wasn't for my plants I think I would have gone stark raving mad a long time ago," he said looking round at his balcony. "By the way, I'm sorry if I was a little short with you earlier but this blinkin' dinner has been giving me a real headache. Usually it's the Embassy that takes care of that sort of thing but this year they're having the place refurbished. I don't mind helping them out but I was only told about it last week."

"We all have our crosses to bear," I replied quietly.

"Quite," Huggins mumbled, as he pawed at a pile of chits on his desk. "So, are you heading down toward South Africa from here?" he asked.

"No, Australia." I replied.

"Never been flying myself. But a colleague of mine down the corridor has his own little aeroplane; he goes flying most weekends. He's taken some marvellous photos of the Pyramids. They're on the wall outside; really stunning they are. He's always inviting me up but I don't think I'd have the stomach for it. I'm always reading about people having mishaps in these contraptions. Oh excuse me," he said, once again berating the receiver. "Hello? Can you hear me? Whose that? It's Huggins here - from P&O."

As ships cruised serenely along the Canal just outside the window, Huggins launched himself into a double declutch of logistical lingo. He began shifting about uncomfortably in the heat and his face developed a lingering crimson, as he was forced to draw up several drafts of the Old Chums' Act.

"...and make sure they get the spelling right on that birthday cake I've ordered for this weekend," he laughed nervously before banging down the receiver. "Right. You're in luck. There's a tanker just come in from Benghazi early this morning," he said looking at me somewhat wearily. "They're supposed to be re-supplying the local RAF base but I've made sure that some of it gets siphoned off for you. I've also thrown in some hampers to tie you over for lunch and dinner and, hopefully, everything should be with you in a couple of hours – or less. Is that OK?"

"Sounds perfect. Thank you very much. And here's my end of the bargain. All done." I said passing him his papers back across the desk.

"Gosh that was quick. Excellent. I don't know about you but I definitely need a drink after that," he said, reaching for a decanter behind his desk.

A generous measure of gin quickly re-floated his composure and he started itemising the bill in calligraphy on a piece of headed foolscap.

"Now, listen, regarding payment," he said, pausing to re-fill his glass. "I can let you have the hampers on the house, so to speak, but I'm going to have to charge you for the petrol. It wasn't easy getting hold of it and I'll probably have to grease a few palms at the end of the day."

"I quite understand," I said, looking forward somewhat squeamishly as he began totting up the numbers on the page. "Will cash do?"

"Yes. Yes. Fine. Never known anyone to turn down cash?" he chuckled, before suddenly looking up. "Actually, come to think of it, there hardly seems any point in me giving you a pro forma now if, as you say, you're going to be stopping here regular like. How many aircraft have you got servicing this route?"

"I'm really not sure exactly, as I say I haven't been with the company very long."

"Well, I'll be happy to sort out all Imperial's supply needs in this part of the world from now on. Just tell them to give me a couple of days' notice and I'll have everything sorted out."

"I'm sure they'd agree to that. Sounds perfect," I replied.

"In the meantime." Huggins said standing up. "I'll just send this invoice to your Offices back in Blighty."

"Perfect," I replied, as we both walked toward the door. "I'm afraid I don't have their address on me, though."

"Don't worry about that. I'm sure our Accounts can sort it out. It's not as if *Imperial Airways* is some fly-by-night operation," he laughed.

I didn't immediately register what he said; probably because I was rather keen to get back and give Ms Hammond the good news. But as I scurried down the stairs, I felt sure that someone somewhere within that vast organisation was bound to correct the mistake; and if they didn't, it certainly wasn't going give Ms Hammond any sleepless nights.

Having hacked my way back through the jungle of hyperbole, I returned to find her ready to greet me at the door.

"You took your time. I've already had to send the passengers away once," she said with a cold rush in her voice. "So did you get anything?"

"Yes, all the fuel and supplies will be arriving in about an hour," I replied, a little out of breath.

"You got both petrol *and* provisions."

"Yes, just as you ordered."

"And the petrol's the correct octane?"

"Yes, I made sure of that. It's proper aviation fuel."

"I see," Ms Hammond replied, as if biting her tongue. "And where did you manage to get all this stuff?"

"From Peninsular and Orient, down by the Canal."

"Oh great. I might as well have 'phoned up 'Harrods'," she said, rolling her eyes like a fruit machine. "I suppose it's a stupid question but do you have any change from the money I gave you?"

"Yes – just a bit," I replied, pulling her cash out of my jacket.

"But this looks like all of it," she said with sullen surprise.

"It is – they'll be sending you an invoice."

"An invoice?" she answered, looking puzzled. "You mean they've given it to us on credit?"

"That's right. The quartermaster at P&O has set up an account for you."

"What - just like that?" Ms Hammond uttered in astonishment. "Without references or bank statements?"

"Yes, from now on, he said, if you need any supplies, just call ahead and he'll have everything ready and prepared."

Ms Hammond screwed up her face and stepped back inside the plane as if needing a sit down.

"Well, this all sounds a bit too good to be true if you ask me," she muttered, shaking her head. "But, I suppose, we'll find out in about an hour or so, won't we? In the meantime you'd better get on and give the engines a quick once over. And check on that repair to the hull as well."

"I thought you wanted me to trade in those two suitcases," I shrugged, feeling somewhat crest-fallen.

"Well, let's wait and see if these supplies turn up shall we?" she said, generously giving me the benefit of the doubt.

It was almost as if she enjoyed watching me stumble, every time I dared take a step up in her estimations. My waking hours now seemed to be comprised of little more than listening to her sadistic rancour, whilst struggling to plug the dyke with all my finger and toes.

When the supplies I had prophesised did arrive, I came down from the wing more out of curiosity than compulsion. I found Ms Hammond standing in the galley surrounded by P&O hampers and I sharpened my mettle in the doorway while I waited for her reaction.

"My God, look at all this stuff!" she said spinning around with a huge grin slapped across her face. "Just look at it! We've got everything: a four course meal, toothpicks - even ice-cream! And it's not just lunch and dinner they've provided us with," she blurted out, interrupting herself. "Look, we've got afternoon tea as well!"

There was an almost tearful glint in her eye as she peered under every lid in turn. Inside, sliced meats were displaying like peacocks and cakes, perched upon trivets, began flirting with the flies the moment they were revealed.

"Goodness me, this is going to make my life so much easier. This is just what we need – a real shot in the arm. I never thought I'd say this - but I'm actually looking forward to doing the serving now," she laughed, before stepping toward me and placing both her hands on my shoulders. "My God, last night I honestly thought maybe the game was up. But I wasn't expecting anything like this. Gosh, I could kiss you. You really have - excelled yourself. Thank you so much."

As I struggled to remain first cousin observant, she looked me in the eye with an honesty that just an hour or so earlier would have been swiftly suffocated. I couldn't help but think that maybe now there would be less left unsaid; and maybe that second half-crown might come in handy after all.

20

The supplies from P&O furnished us with more than just a feeling of triumph and optimism. Maybe it was only a stay of execution, but I no longer felt like an ill-fitting tenant or a piano player caught up in a bar-room brawl. As I climbed back up onto the wing to supervise the re-fuelling, Ms Hammond seemed freed from the straight-laced idiocy that everyone demanded. She welcomed the passengers back on board with a calm, valeted lilt, instead of the cauterised croak you might expect from a nun, gasping for a brandy.

Unfortunately the passengers didn't quite share this new found spirit of anticipation. They marched on board beneath leaden hats and gruff burblings, concerning a variety of issues.

"So much for defending my honour, or any other part of me for that matter," Campari scowled at her other half, as he trailed behind her along the pier. "That man almost knocked me off my feet when he tried to grab my necklace. And what did you do? Absolutely nothing. Although I suppose I'm lucky to have any jewellery at all, after the amount you spent in the bar and that roulette table."

It was a perfect exhibition of irate and inert and our remaining prodigals rolled up displaying remarkably similar symptoms.

"And I'll be watching you on this next flight. You can

order one drink and that's all," the Blunderbuss muttered to her companion. "I know exactly what you were up to the last time – looking down that stewardess's blouse indeed. Disgusting."

The general air of discord ruffled my repose but it didn't bother Ms Hammond. As soon as the re-fuelling was done, she welcomed me back into the cockpit as if I'd just slid down a beanstalk.

"Right then," she said, spilling a careless smile, which I cautiously shared. "I'd better show you the route for the next leg – if I'm going to be serving in the cabin."

She pulled out a chart that, once again, illustrated just another huge, vacuous area.

"This is where we're heading next, Bandar Kangan. It's just here on the other side of the Persian Gulf. The goings a little trickier this time, though, because there'll be no landmarks for most of it. What you'll need to do is follow this railway line all the way across the desert."

"Looks fairly straightforward," I said confidently.

"Yes, well, unfortunately things aren't quite that simple because stretches of the line don't exist anymore; I think we've got Lawrence of Arabia and his chums to thank for that. But as soon as you lose sight of it, make a note of your compass heading and then simply hold that course and hopefully it should just re-appear. Got that?"

I had had enough navigational instruction to know that, even with the best maps, it usually involved about three parts art to one part science.

"I see. So we just rely on the instruments and trust our luck." I said, trying not to cringe.

"Yes that's about it," she replied nonchalantly. "By the way, do you know how to take a star fix?"

"No, I'm afraid not."

"Well, that makes two of us. What about night flying, have you done much of that?"

"It's not my forte." I confessed. "Are we not going to get there before nightfall then?"

"Well, no, not now," she said looking at her watch. "we're leaving a good bit later than I would have liked. But at least we've got plenty of fuel and supplies, hey?" she concluded with a grin.

I almost felt as though I were suffering from a tired joke as she handed me the chart; I climbed into my seat and found myself scanning for the gauge that would show exactly how much good fortune needed to be factored into that leg of the flight. But, emancipated from such concerns, Ms Hammond fired up the engines, before relinquishing the controls almost as soon as we were airborne; she left me alone in the cockpit, gawping at a pair of steel rails that shone like a beacon in the sunlight.

It became a blinding monotony that conspired with the heat to give our machine a barely discernible speed. We seemed to leave nothing behind except the occasional goods train, ploughing through the sand. Double-headed anthracite mules churned up almighty palls, which rose like flocks of ammonites. But the moment they disappeared beneath us, we reverted back to the same lazy drift upon an alabaster ocean, whose passionless stare had me longing for Ms Hammond's return.

I consoled myself with all the things she had said to me earlier and the broad smile that had accompanied those words. I was no longer just another conceited concoction, moulded by men who slept with their hands outside the sheets. I even dared to contemplate a future where we might be on more familiar terms. I conjured up a few possible first names for her; but they all sounded rather colourless and ordinary, like a crowd holding hands in a blurring downpour.

It was the only pleasant distraction from the isolation pasted across the glass. When we entered the Arabian peninsula I simply sat ticking off places that existed solely in theory or had long since disappeared beneath the creep of the dunes; their serpentine skins flaked off in the wind and, just as Ms Hammond had predicted, the railway line would disappear beneath the desert for miles at a time. With only so much accuracy to be had from shuddering dials, I simply had to sit and wait anxiously for the track to reappear.

Almost inevitably my thoughts turned to engine failures and other mishaps, which were teased out by the high mileage I knew the plane had clocked up. Its best years had probably been spent cruising around Caribbean atolls. But now, with the load we were carrying, I didn't hold out much hope of remaining airborne if one of the engines suddenly conked out. Nor did there seem to be much chance of any rescue, in the event of a forced landing. The only sign of life I spotted during the entire flight was a couple of Bedouin caravans. But, wrapped in their highwayman headgear, they appeared to congregate like dorsal fins around watering holes. They didn't wave at us when we flew past, as I was used to seeing; they merely stared up and pointed with what looked like Lee-Enfield rifles.

For hour after hour I was forced to consider how far we were standing in harm's way. I watched as skeletal shapes laddered the barren above us and ghostly spouts of dust emerged from the Bauhaus scenery. They promenaded across the screen, twinkling like nebulae in the heat of the sun and their alluring contortions seemed to draw us forward with gentle dust-pan gusts. At first it was a benign spectacle: eager eddies simply skipped across the control surfaces. But soon the wind picked up and the ride became increasingly rough. As the horizon started to diminish, my hands began chipping paint from the controls. I watched the desert slowly raise itself up like a monument, obliterating the view and I was left staring in awe at the sheer scale of the sandstorm ahead of us.

Unsure as to how much fuel we had to spare, there seemed no alternative except to head straight towards it; although I shuddered at the chaos it would cause the carburettor jets and the thousands of moving parts. But, as I peered forwards almost transfixed, the cockpit door suddenly slammed behind me and Ms Hammond jumped into her seat. She immediately grabbed hold of the column and pushed open the throttles to full boost. We began a sharp, spiralling ascent with the pulse of the plane smearing all the instruments and the propellers spinning like fluid in the heat. Every component became wired for sound as she heaved with gritted teeth. I sat feeling utterly disposable, waiting for the order to start throwing out anything that wasn't screwed down. But, at about 15,000ft she finally levelled off and brought the nose back round to our original compass bearing. Ahead of us, the sky was once again perfectly clear; the railway line, however, was now far below us, completely out of sight.

21

We seemed to hover, far from any Earthly scrutiny where the air was thin and cold. A screaming thirst clawed at my neck and my shoes began biting around my ankles. The instruments still vied for my attention but now they all appeared strangely distant and trivial; there wasn't any mortality to be concerned with anymore, until I glanced across and saw blood coming out of Ms Hammond's ear.

For some reason, it seemed to take an age to get her attention and, even then, she just stared at me, blinking with gormless indifference. I pointed to the side of her head and shouted but she simply sat looking mildly insulted. Eventually, out of sheer frustration, I dabbed my handkerchief against her ear and she reared back in shock as soon as she saw it. She jumped up out of her seat and disappeared behind me, while I grabbed hold of the controls.

I expected her to be back within moments - and when she didn't return I assumed she had gone aft to tend to the passengers; I pictured them all tucking into yet another sumptuous banquet while she fluttered about them like a fairy. No one was competing for her affections any more; there was just a buoyancy and warmth enveloping the vessel. I could feel it through my hands as we floated along, quietly gurgling upon the abundance of fuel.

It was only as the sun began to set that I started to

wonder if we were still on the right course and I glanced down at the map; but it was just a baffling tartan of gridlines and weather patterns. Everything now looked perfectly clear around us, so I pushed the column forward to try and pick up the railway line again. As the aircraft slowly descended, however, darkness settled upon the sand below, cruelly robbing us of our guiding star. Luck, once again, seemed to be refereeing the scene and my fingers chafed the controls like a rosary while I waited for Ms Hammond to come and vanquish the gloom.

But there was no sudden exorcism when she did finally return to her seat. She just sat slumped with her arms shawled around her, clutching a handkerchief against her mouth. She showed no interest in any of the instruments, so I assumed we were still on the correct heading; although, as her ghostly profile lingered beside me, my glances toward her began to feel more like a vigil. She simply kept staring dead ahead while I sat biting at scanty illuminations; there was no beauty to be enjoyed and the wretched emptiness droned on until, finally, a large body of water appeared, shimmering beneath the moonlight. I raised my head up like an ostrich, knowing that this had to be the Persian Gulf and Bandar Kangan lay somewhere to starboard over on the other side.

Without even looking at me, however, Ms Hammond immediately took hold of the controls and pulled the aircraft round to port. No matter how far off course we might have drifted, this was completely the wrong direction and I quickly turned to her holding the map up in my hand. But, with an almost trance-like nod, she sedated my authority as navigator. There was no explanation; she simply continued on a north westerly course, following the shoreline.

It seemed as though our recent détente had counted for nothing and we each reverted back to our own frigid isolation: she strained forward in her seat, occasionally kneading her eyes, while I leaned against the fuselage, wondering where on Earth we were going to end up. I folded the map away and waited patiently for another port or harbour to emerge from the blackness. Sure enough, it eventually appeared in the distance, throbbing beneath the haloed glow of yet more bothersome people and biting insects.

Ms Hammond dutifully headed towards it, along a wide estuary marked out by a trail of coloured beacons. When we were still some way off, however, she suddenly banked the aircraft and started to orbit what looked like a large lake. As we slowly circled, she peered down the nose and began comparing notes with the view out of the side screen; I had no idea what she was looking for - nor did I show much interest, until she pulled the flare gun out from under her seat. To my astonishment, she fired a shot through the window and, almost immediately, a vessel of some sort erupted in a blaze of light below us. A flare path beside it then unzipped the darkness like a billboard and, without any hesitation, Ms Hammond swooped down upon it. The hull seemed to chuckle on the water's cusp as we surfed toward a double-decker houseboat, which sat splendidly assured with keepsake railings and frivolous paintwork.

As we approached, a team of natives came flapping out through the door, clad in white linens. They tied us up to an adjoining walkway before assembling like a chorus line at the end of the gangplank.

"We made it. Thank God for that," Ms Hammond sighed, burying her face in her hands.

"This place looks rather grand," I remarked through the window, as one of the staff opened the cabin door while the rest incongruously erected parasols. "Where exactly are we, though?" I finally enquired. "Just in case any of the passengers should ask."

"Al-Basrah," Ms Hammond replied in a muffled voice.

"Pardon me?"

"Basra," she said, lifting her head slightly. "It's on the Persian Mesopotamian border."

"I see. So - may I ask what happened to Bandar Kangan?"

"I don't think we'd have had enough juice to get there, not after we ran into that sandstorm. And besides I didn't fancy my chances of finding it in the dark. But I know *Imperial Airways* have night-landing facilities at all their stops."

"Oh, so this place doesn't belong to you then?"

"God no. I haven't even been here before. I just hope they don't mind us dropping in on them like this. It doesn't look too bad, though, does it?" she said peering over the control column. "I hope they've got some decent facilities. I'm dying to have a bath – and a pee," she added, before reaching down to take a drink from her flask. "Go on now, please. I'll be along in a minute. Explain to everyone that we've stopped here purely as a precaution - you know, in the name of safety and all that lark."

Once again, she refused to give me so much as a sideways glance as she dished out her orders. But I obediently complied, despite feeling pretty whacked out after almost twelve hours of flying. As I got up out of my seat, however, I was surprised to see one of her shoes lying discarded near the back of the cockpit.

"Is this yours?" I enquired, picking it up.

"What is it?" Ms Hammond replied sharply.

She only turned a little in her seat but the lights from the houseboat illuminated her face. At first, I just noticed that her make-up was smeared; but, as I handed her her shoe, I was shocked to see that both her eyes were badly swollen and there was blood on her blouse.

"My God, Ms Hammond," I gasped. "What happened to you?"

"What? Oh, nothing, I'm fine," she said bending away from me like a sapling.

"But your face? Are you alright?"

"Yes, yes. I just slipped on some oil back there, that's all. Must have banged my head on something. Nothing to worry about."

"I'll go and get some ice for you," I said spinning around in panic.

"No, no. Please, it's just a bump. Go and see to the passengers now. As I say, I'll be along in a few minutes. Oh and make sure they get some dinner - I didn't get a chance to serve any."

But the passengers certainly weren't a priority from where I was standing and I found myself gazing around the cockpit in post mortem. All I could see was her slender body lying spread-eagled behind me - and even now, her head seemed to be floundering upon her shoulders. With her swan neck gone, she curled in her seat as if withering under the scrutiny of the lights. It was like watching a fox going to ground and I flung open the cockpit door, unable to look on any longer. I dashed through into the cabin which, mercifully, was now completely empty. As I stepped outside, however, I was confronted by a half-dressed maitre d', who stood hopping about in front of me as if he'd just shot himself in the foot.

"We are not expecting you today," he said breathlessly, holding his timetable aloft. "Look!"

"Yes, I'm terribly sorry," I apologised in a daze, "but we ran into a spot of bad weather and had to make a slight detour."

"But we have nothing prepared!" he said, still in a state of flambé.

"Yes, well, as I say, I'm very sorry about that," I muttered, glancing over his shoulder. "Listen, you wouldn't happen to have a doctor on board that thing would you?" I asked, pointing toward the houseboat.

"A doctor?" he replied, somewhat startled. "No. Why? Are you sick?"

"Not me, no," I replied. "What about some ice? Do you think you could get me some ice?"

"Ice? Yes, of course. Please. Come. This way."

He scampered back toward the houseboat, still assembling his collar. But, as he opened the door, he was instantly confronted by a mob of panic-stricken kitchen staff. They began furiously gobbling like pheasants under fire until, finally, the maitre d' simply threw up his hands and let out a scream, before disappearing towards the stern. It was all somewhat at odds with the slick, fragrant hospitality I had been expecting: the entire vessel and its crew seemed to be creaking and groaning as the ladies trooped upstairs, while the men set upon a bar near the bow. Despite feeling somewhat abandoned, I nevertheless conformed to this voluntary segregation and I stepped up to the bar, still hoping to get hold of some ice for Ms Hammond.

"It's buffet service - if it's a drink you want," her brother-in-law smiled at me from the other end.

"Oh – right," I said, glancing around in vain for a bar tender. "Marvellous."

"I'm not complaining. Here, have a drink on me," he

laughed, passing me a bottle of champagne. "Is the Skipper not going to be joining us?"

"No, no," I sighed, moving slowly towards him. "Actually she doesn't seem to be feeling too well."

"Nothing serious I hope."

"To be honest, I'm not quite sure. I was just hoping to get some ice for her - she's got this almighty bump on her head."

"How did that happen?"

"I don't know exactly. She said she slipped and bashed it on something. But, quite frankly, when I saw her just now, I thought she'd been in a fight."

"Wouldn't surprise me with her," he smirked. "Although, I was wondering why she suddenly stopped serving the drinks."

"She says she's fine, of course. But, I have to say, I really am quite worried about her."

"Well," he said looking at me a little more intently. "I don't usually advertise but in a previous life I used to be a doctor – if you want me to take a look at her."

Having heard Ms Hammond's opinion of him, I had to hesitate before embracing his offer.

"Well - that would certainly put my mind at ease. Thank you. I would appreciate it."

"I'm not sure if she'll feel the same way, though," he smiled. "If I'm going to examine her, I'll probably need someone to hold her down. We don't always see eye to eye."

"At the moment I'd be surprised if she can see anything at all - her face is so swollen up."

"Oh, it's that bad, is it? Where is she now?"

"Still in the cockpit. Although, she said she was going to go and take a bath."

"Well, I tell you what, leave it with me and in about an hour or so, I'll go and knock on her door," he said placing his hand on my arm. "You look pretty bushed yourself. Why don't you turn in for the night? There's no need for you to be hanging around here, standing on ceremony. I think we can all look after ourselves."

"It's tempting but I wouldn't mind getting something to eat."

"Well, I think you could be in for a bit of a wait -" he uttered, before being interrupted by a loud bang which extinguished all the lights.

An almighty commotion of shrieks and yelps erupted on the deck above; but the men around me went on nesting in their wingbacks, calmly warming their brandies by the light from their cigars.

"I say, this is just like something from an Agatha Christie novel, isn't it?" the Blunderbuss's companion chuckled. "Shall we all play murder in the dark?"

"Wait for my wife to come down and we can do it for real," the Tweedy Gent answered.

The room filled with rapturous laughter but I didn't find the humour particularly infectious; all I could think of was Ms Hammond languishing alone inside the aircraft. As I looked out at the lights in the cabin still burning brightly, another nagging concern also lingered in the shadows; I couldn't help but wonder if, maybe, I should have been a little more reticent with her brother-in-law.

"Say," he then enquired quietly. "you don't fancy a swim, do you?"

"A swim?" I replied, a little taken aback. "What out there - in the lake?"

"Yes, why not? It's a bit stuffy in here. I fancy cooling off a bit."

"Well, that's nice of you to offer," I said, straightening up, "but I suppose, strictly speaking, I'm still on duty - and I doubt if her ladyship would want to see me frolicking around in the buff."

"Suit yourself," he shrugged, before turning to address the rest of the room. "Here, any of lot fancy joining me for a swim?"

"That's not a bad idea," Soda responded. "Not much fun sitting here in the dark - we can't even have a game of cards."

"Yes, and I could do with a bath," the Tweedy gent added.

"Come on then. Fall in," Ms Hammond's brother-in-law commanded, before tripping toward the door.

To my amazement, everyone followed him outside, where they all began stripping off. He liberated one of the mooring buoys from the side of the houseboat and an impromptu game of water polo ensued. It was a little odd, at first, watching them all splashing about like toddlers - and their antics certainly didn't go down very well with the maitre d'. As soon as the lights had been restored he came steaming into the bar:

"Dinner is ready, sir," he puffed triumphantly, before glancing around the room. "But - where has everybody gone?"

"They're outside," I replied.

"Outside?"

"Yes, they're all having a swim."

"What? No, no, they must not do that," he said rushing up to the window. "No, no, no, no, no."

He thundered back out through the door and I followed close behind to see what all the fuss was about.

"Please, gentlemen, please. Come in quickly," he shouted from the walkway, beckoning everyone towards him.

"What the devil's the matter old boy?" the Tweedy Gent called out.

"You must come in. It is not safe. There are crocodiles."

"Crocodiles, did you say?"

"Yes, many, many crocodiles. You must come in," the maitre d' wailed.

"How big are these crocodiles exactly?" Ms Hammond's brother-in-law shouted back.

"What, does it matter?" the maitre d' cried, waving his

arms in the air. "Please, sir. Gentlemen. The dinner is ready. Please come in."

"Alright. Don't panic. We'll be in in a minute and if we see any crocodiles, we'll give you a shout and you can tell us what to do."

"Yes, I fancy a nice new wallet," the Blunderbuss's companion laughed, as the game of water polo calmly resumed.

Seemingly unable to look on any longer, the maitre d' spun around and gazed at me, almost in tears.

"These English, do they not know about crocodiles?"

"I suspect most of them do," I replied.

"So, are they just mad?" he whimpered

"You know, I really wouldn't like to say."

"Well - " he said glancing up to the heavens. "I can do no more. They are in God's hands now. Please Captain, sir. The dinner is ready. Please come with me."

I was certainly less willing to trust in providence but, nonetheless, followed him back to the houseboat, just as the ladies were coming down in their cocktail fatigues. We all filed into the dining room where the mirrors and marquetry seemed to pander to the strapless wonders, while ignoring the rankled tweeds. The maitre d' guided me to a table in the centre of the room, while the ladies drifted slowly in a rudderless mass toward the windows.

"Looks as if I'll be eating alone again tonight," Campari remarked bitterly.

"I think most of us will," the Dusky Mistress added, as they all stood gazing outside. "Unless, of course, we can join you at the Captain's table," she then asked, turning towards me.

In all honesty, that was the last thing I wanted; but a sorry huddle of eyes seemed to peep out from behind the wall of staunch veneers.

"Of course, madam." I said, addressing them collectively. "I'd be delighted."

"Thank you. It's a pleasure to be in the company of a proper gentleman," the Dusky Mistress replied taking a seat next to me. "I was beginning to wonder if there were any left."

"And may I sit here?" the Blunderbuss enquired, positioning herself on the other side of me. "Or is that charming stewardess going to be joining us?"

"No, I don't think she'll be making another appearance tonight," I replied.

"Thank goodness for that," she said, sitting down. "Because her manners are quite appalling. I shall be writing a stern letter about her to the management when I get back to England. She seems to treat us all like a minor inconvenience. Tell me, how long have you had young girls like that flying with you?"

"To be honest, madam, I'm not quite sure. I'm fairly new myself," I explained.

"Well, she's not going to last long. A swift court martial back at Southampton. That's what's needed."

"I can have her walking the plank at first light tomorrow, if you like," I suggested.

"There's no need to be facetious," the Blunderbuss scowled at me, before peering across at the Dusky Mistress who was already smirking into her soup.

"I do apologise madam but I believe that this is only her first flight and, perhaps, she's taking a little time to acclimatise to the thin air."

"Thin air? Is that what you call it?" she blustered. "Because on more than one occasion I'm sure I smelled strong spirits on her breath."

Her nagging dogma continued to well like an abscess, while I sat adjudicating the finish of the monogrammed cutlery. Only the arrival of the main course curtailed her contempt for Ms Hammond and her face seemed to drop like a bomb as a grey, pullet chicken landed in front of her.

"Goodness me," she said, scrutinising the accompanying vegetables, which looked as though they'd been boiled tasteless in a muslin sack. "I was hardly expecting standards on this vessel to rival the *Queen Mary* but, really – this looks barely edible."

"I quite agree," Campari said, before glancing round as the men began raucously emerging from the lake. "Mind you, that's a sight to put anyone off their food."

"And I don't suppose any of them will have the decency to join us for dinner," the Tweedy Gent's wife muttered.

"They shouldn't even be allowed back on board, unless they're suitably attired," the Blunderbuss insisted without looking up.

"That might be wishful thinking," the Dusky Mistress said with a wry smile as a gaggle of naked bodies streaked past the door.

"Well, at least none of them were eaten by the crocodiles," I remarked with a quiet smile.

"Serves them right if they were," Campari snapped back, almost spitting out the words.

From then on, even the most benign generalities, uttered purely in the name of fair play, were quickly dramatised by a rampant pitch. Voices splashed through me like a reflection in a puddle as the free-flowing booze sketched out men in caricature. Their indiscretions and nuisances were then horse-traded across the table, while I sat sweating on the inside, as if someone had placed an apple on my head.

"Oh goodness. Isn't there anything better we can talk about - other than just gossiping about our husbands," the Dusky Mistress finally gasped, before looking towards me. "You must think we're all such frightful bores, Captain."

"Oh no, not at all," I replied. "Please. Carry on."

"Well I think it's awfully good of you to stay up and look after us like this. After all, you must be exhausted, having spent all day flying that big aeroplane, all by yourself."

"Yes, I have been meaning to ask you about that," the Blunderbuss interjected. "Are there not supposed to be two pilots on a long flight like this?"

"Well," I said cranking myself round the other way, "there has been quite a lot of cost cutting within the company recently. But I suppose everyone's feeling the pinch at the moment."

"Still," the Dusky Mistress said, placing her hand on my shoulder. "It must get awfully lonely sitting in that cockpit for hour after hour with nothing to do except wiggle that joystick – or whatever it is you do with it."

"Oh, it's not so bad," I replied. "The stewardess comes in from time to time to keep me company. She likes to keep me on my toes."

"Oh really? And how does she do that, may I ask?"

"Oh, you know, with cups of tea - and the odd sandwich."

"Is that all?" the Dusky Mistress enquired further, with her jewellery winking at me. "Doesn't she have any other talents?"

"My needs are, really, quite straightforward," I tried to re-assure her.

"So are mine," she smiled, before raising her glass in the air for yet another re-fill. "Still, I'm sure you'd rather be cosying up to her right now, rather than listening to us prattling on about our problems. She is rather pretty after all, isn't she? Don't you think she's pretty?"

"Well - " I stuttered.

"I think she's very pretty - if a little grumpy. But the

pretty ones always are, aren't they?" she laughed, nudging me with her elbow.

"Her culinary skills could certainly do with some improvement," the Blunderbuss butted in again.

"Oh for Heaven's sake! Is that the only way to judge a woman? Shame on you," the Dusky Mistress cried.

She tipped back her wine glass once more but her bosom suddenly lost all proportion as her dress slipped down a couple of inches.

"What about love – and passion?" she went on regardless. "Isn't that important?"

"I think you've been reading too many Bronte novels," the Blunderbuss uttered.

"Nonsense! You haven't given it a chance."

"Well, I think we'll have to agree to disagree on this occasion because, if you don't mind, I'm going to retire for the night," the Blunderbuss said getting up.

"Yes, I think I'll do likewise," the Tweedy Gent's wife added. "I'm not sure if my constitution can endure another course."

Most of the chairs around the table then began coughing as their occupants made their excuses in turn, before joining a train of clacking heels led by the Blunderbuss.

The Dusky Mistress, however, remained in her seat, seemingly smouldering with condescension as she fired up a cigarette.

"Not much point in me going to bed. There won't be

there," she growled. "I'll bet you £10 he's not in ᴊom," she added with a look of purpose in her steely

"I'm not really a betting man," I confessed, wincing at ᴄhe amount.

"Alright make it £10 both ways. Can't say fairer than that," she said grasping hold of my hand.

"I really wouldn't have thought there's too far you can wander on a little boat like this." I said, doing my best to console her.

"Oh you'd be amazed the nooks and crannies that man can worm his way into," she muttered, before examining me a little closer. "But you – you seem like a good man. Are you good?"

"I have my moments." I replied.

"And are you spoken for? Or do you have a girl in every port?" she smirked, placing her hand on my thigh.

"Well this is only my first trip, so I haven't had much of a chance to get to know any of the locals - so to speak."

"Well, there's still time," she giggled. "We're only halfway to Australia."

"And are you going all the way?" I enquired, triggering a dark smile that illuminated her eyes.

"I beg your pardon?"

"To Darwin, that is."

"Oh heavens no. Nothing goes to Darwin except the mail," she said, looking disparagingly around the table. "I'm getting off at Singapore, as usual."

"Oh so this isn't your first time flying with us then?"

"I should think not," she hooted. "Do you not kno who I am?"

I gazed at her helplessly, whilst she bathed herself in a hollow eminence which I pretended not to notice.

"Goodness me, you really are rather green aren't you?" she sniggered. "Have you not heard of Sir Stanley Ricardo?"

"I'm afraid not, no, madam. I'm sorry."

"Quite the charmer aren't you? Well, let me enlighten you. He's the largest rubber exporter in all of the Malayan peninsular."

"Goodness," I smiled politely.

"Why don't you ask him for a job. You look as if you could do with some colour in your cheeks."

"Is he looking for a pilot?"

"Well he can fly, but he's not very good. In fact, he's just bought himself a new plane. A 'Puss Moth' I think it's called. Probably explains why he can't fly it," she snorted.

"And do you fly?"

"Oh no, of course not," she scoffed. "Although I sometimes wish I could. The roads in Malaya are so bad - especially during the monsoon. In fact, I rather like flying. It's the coming back down to Earth I can't stand."

She pressed herself back into her seat as if being whisked along with the wind in her hair. But a discordant mutter of voices above us then seemed to steal her gaze and nce - until a yawn finally got the better of

"...or goodness sake, aren't you going to have ...k?" she suddenly erupted - as her face split like ...o panes.

'I do apologise, Lady Ricardo."

"Really. You don't drink, don't smoke, don't gamble. ...u are good aren't you? A little too good. Just my luck," she shrugged, before slumping forwards across the table.

"I'm sorry to be a bore - but these early starts are catching up with me."

"Well I can tell you now, there's not much point in going to bed because the mattresses on board this thing are as hard as nails."

"Anything's an improvement over the cockpit floor," I muttered quietly.

"What?" she said, looking up. "You mean you've been sleeping on board the plane?"

"All part of the company's latest economy drive, I believe."

"Why, that's outrageous. What a shoddy way to treat one's employees. The least you should expect is a decent night's rest after a long day of flying," she said thumping the table. "Well, next stop you stick with me. I'll make sure you're alright. 'H' is getting off at Karachi anyway, so I'll need someone to keep me company," she winked. "You've got a room here for tonight, though?"

"Yes. I believe so."

"Well then, let's get you upstairs, you poor dab. You must be exhausted."

Taking hold of my hand as though it were a paw, we swayed gently up the stairs. On the upper deck was a long dark corridor punctuated by louvered doors, with a porter sitting fast asleep at the far end.

"Right then, Captain. Here are my quarters," Lady Ricardo sighed, before letting go of my hand. "I'd better bid you goodnight."

"Oh. Yes. Goodnight, Lady Ricardo," I said with a slight bow as she threw open her bedroom door and switched on the light.

"See, what did I tell you? No one here," she declared, pointing to an empty four-poster bed. "It's been a good night for you though, hasn't it?" she added with a smile, before plucking a £10 note from her clutch purse.

"Oh no, really, Lady Ricardo. I couldn't," I insisted as she waved it like a fragrance in front of my nose.

"No, a bet's a bet. And you won fair and square. So - there you are. £10. Less commission of course."

As she slipped it into my top pocket, she grasped hold of my lapels and pressed her lips against my face. Her flesh bubbled up against me and her perfume suspended any thoughts or beliefs. When, finally, she released me, her hands slithered across my chest and she seemed to disappear inside her room behind a melancholy fog. For a brief moment, I did wonder if there was anything else I could do for her; but good governance quickly returned when I glanced around and saw the porter standing up. He looked at me with a gracious understanding as if he'd witnessed the spectacle so many times before. But all I felt was the indignity of having strayed into a world which I had come to despise. It shared nothing with Ms Hammond's noble philosophy of ambition and triumph and I simply wanted to run to her and explain myself – giving up every last detail.

"Excuse me, sir," the porter finally murmured as he crept toward me, hugging the skirting board. "There is a room for you - just here."

"Thank you," I uttered, following him to the last door along the corridor, where I was greeted by the sight of snow-white bed linen lying beneath a silken mosquito net.

"I do hope everything is to your liking."

"Yes. It all looks wonderful." I replied.

"And would you like your clothes to be laundered – ready for the morning?"

"Oh no, no," I shrugged, before glancing down at my tunic and the finger marks which may or may not have been there. "Although, maybe, it could do with a clean."

There was a screen in the corner of the room but it looked a long way away. So, in something of a daze, I simply stripped off down to my smalls, while the porter looked on, ashen faced. As soon as I handed him my uniform, he scurried out of the room and I never saw the poor man again. Although with hindsight, I suppose, it was understandable given that he had already witnessed half the passengers strutting around stark naked.

I collapsed on top of the bed which, thankfully, was a good deal more compliant than Lady Ricardo's insistences. But, as I settled down for the night, the entire bedstead cackled vociferously with tell-tale creaks that seemed to be taunting me for what I had or, perhaps, hadn't done. The chorus of disapproval was soon joined by a shriek from the room next door.

"Ow! That bloody hurt H," Ms Hammond cried out in agony.

"For God's sake Cess. Just keep still and stop complaining," her brother-in-law said in a furious whisper as I pressed my ear against the wall.

"Don't call me Cess," she replied angrily, almost spelling out the word.

"It's either Cess or Silly. One or the other."

"Cecily is bad enough. Just stick to that."

"Alright, alright. But will you please come a little further into the light. I need to get a better look at you."

"Oh what does it matter – there's nothing you can do. Just give me something to get rid of my headache. I'm sure I'll be better in the morning."

"Don't be so sure. There's an awful lot of swelling. I wouldn't be at all surprised if you've fractured something."

"And so what if I have?"

"Then you won't be fit to fly tomorrow."

"And who's going to stop me? You?" she snorted. "Besides I haven't got much choice, have I? I can hardly serve in the cabin looking like this."

"What about the rest of your crew? Where the hell are they, may I ask?"

"I've had to make some cut backs lately, haven't I."

"I'd heard you were going through a rough patch. But I didn't think things were that bad."

"They're not *that* bad. We're doing fine."

"Sure you are, the skipper's half blind and your co-pilot looks barely old enough to drive."

"Leave him out of it. He's alright. And he's a good pilot to boot."

"Well, tomorrow I think you should leave the flying to him."

"Oh listen to you," Ms Hammond scoffed, "the voice of restraint and reason."

"For God's sake, Cecily, there's a real danger that you could just black out."

"Well, I'm sure you've got some special pills to make sure that doesn't happen."

"Here. I'll give you these – and that's all."

"Your sunglasses?"

"Now you can serve in the cabin, problem solved."

"You miserable bastard," Ms Hammond spat as something clattered across the floor. "You know, you really make me sick. You don't seem to mind doping my sister and her friends up to the eyeballs. But when it comes to actually helping someone out, you're bloody useless."

"Alright. Keep your voice down. I'll give you something for your headache."

"What about some sleeping pills as well. God knows I haven't slept properly in days."

"OK. OK," he said rooting around amongst some bottles. "But be careful with these. They're very strong, so just take one at a time."

"Thank you," Ms Hammond conceded. "God knows, I could do with some of these for the passengers."

"I wouldn't have thought drugging your customers would be good for business."

"You don't seem to have a problem with it."

"That's just a bit of fun - between consenting adults," he said quietly. "Besides, you're lot seem pretty quiet after they've had a few drinks."

"It's the tee-totallers I have a problem with. Self-righteous shits. For them, I'm just a nippy in a teahouse."

"Oh, they're not that bad."

"Yes they are. You've seen what they're like when I'm traipsing up and down the aisle."

"Well, listen, why don't you let me help you out tomorrow? I could do some of the serving. I look pretty good in a dickie bow," he laughed.

"No thanks, I'll be fine," she said walking across the

room. "You'd better get back to your floozy before you're missed."

"If you must know, she's just an old acquaintance – and I'm her chaperone, that's all," he said moving toward the door.

"Yes, yes. I'm sure."

"Well, can I get you anything else?"

"No, no I'll be fine."

"Remember, if you're not feeling well in the night. Just come and knock on my door. I'm only down the corridor."

"I wouldn't dream of it. Thank you. Goodnight."

"Good night - and, as I say, take it easy with those pills."

22

I awoke amid a haze of golden gossamer the next morning as sunlight broke into my room. It illuminated my mosquito net and, for a while, I simply lay listening to the dowels and dovetails creaking like birdsong - until the plumbing started banging on the walls. I retrieved my clothes from outside the door and saw a fistful of passengers already standing in a queue outside the bathroom. But as they waited silently in their silk robes and slippers, they all looked quite harmless, like out-patients from an asylum.

It was quiet in the room next door, so I assumed Miss Hammond had risen before dawn, in accordance with her regime. When I looked out of the window, however, the aircraft was still stewing peacefully on the lake with all its apertures firmly closed. As insects swirled around it in a mist, it sat like a cruel reminder that this was all just a fleeting interlude. But, at least, I felt a rejuvenated pride as I trotted downstairs to breakfast in my freshly-pressed uniform.

The maitre d' and his minions were rather more composed than the night before and were standing to attention, ready to ladle out copious amounts of hospitality. There was no one else at breakfast, so I was the sole focus for their withering subservience. The night before I had been a reluctant understudy for Ms Hammond's authority; but now, with staff scurrying around me, it was difficult not to re-adopt the posture of 'Captain'. So I duly received a convoy of domed chargers, before watching in awe as my tea was served with the same reverence as that of wine or champagne.

Any lingering qualms I still felt about being an uninvited guest quickly ebbed away - until a big, black barge approached from the other side of the lake. A figure was standing like a mascot on the prow and, as it drew closer, I could see he was clad in Imperial Airways' regalia. He leapt out of the barge when it was barely alongside the pier and was quickly followed by a team of mechanics. They immediately began casting their eye over our machine, so I raced outside before they could draw too many conclusions.

"Good morning." I called out with a jaunty wave.

"Yes, likewise," a tall, immaculately groomed obelisk muttered from beneath his cap; it was embroidered with the words 'Station Superintendent' and sat at the summit of a seamless tunic that looked as though it had been welded across the cut. "I was told that we had some unexpected arrivals last night," he went on, keeping his hands behind his back.

"Yes, I am so sorry about all this." I replied. "But we ran into a sandstorm and there just wasn't enough fuel for us to make our scheduled stop."

"Quite frankly, I'm amazed you managed to get this far," he said, wincing at the oily streaks soiling the side of the fuselage. "Never thought I'd see one of these again - Consolidated Commodore, isn't it?"

"Yes. That's right."

"I flew one once, a few years back when I was on a secondment to Pan American. This one seems to have picked up a little extra ventilation, though," he smirked, pointing up at some holes in the wing.

"Gosh, yes, I hadn't noticed those before." I said, stepping forward to take a closer look. "I wonder how that happened."

"My dear boy - those are bullet holes," he said, raising one eyebrow like a cat.

"Bullet holes!" I exclaimed. "Are you sure?"

"Well, it's definitely not woodworm," he remarked and all the mechanics around him laughed. "I'd say you've upset someone on your travels. Don't worry, though, my boys here will do their best to repair it. OK chaps get cracking," he said, scattering his men with a clap of his hands. "Check everything over and jet the carburettors, just in case they've picked up some sand in the pipes."

"But we won't have any of the right parts," one of them said. "These aren't Bristol engines, like we've got, sir."

"Just do the best you can," he replied sharply, before turning back to me. "Have you had breakfast?"

"Oh yes, thank you."

"Well, it's never too early for a drink, is it?" he said, leading me back toward the houseboat with his hand on my shoulder. "So where are you heading next?"

"I believe it was supposed to be Karachi," I replied.

"You won't make Karachi, not from here," he said,

shaking his head. "Why don't we ask your Captain? Just to be sure," he said, peering in through the dining room windows. "Is he in here somewhere?"

"No - no," I said hesitantly. "I – I don't think he's got up yet."

"Not got up yet?" the Station Superintendent uttered in amazement.

Before he could say anything else, however, Ms Hammond stormed out of the houseboat, wearing a pair of men's sunglasses. She staggered at speed toward the plane, where she proceeded to grapple with the cabin door.

"What on Earth is that?" he said, as if he were staring at an apparition.

"Oh that's our - flight attendant," I replied.

"You mean to say you have women working aboard your aircraft?"

"Yes, that's right."

"Good God!" He exclaimed. "And did you lot have a party here last night or something?"

"No, no," I assured him, "although the hospitality was excellent."

"Must have been – if your flight attendant can barely walk straight and your Captain's still asleep."

We both watched as Ms Hammond continued to struggle with the cabin door until, eventually, one of the mechanics climbed down from the wing to help her. As he reached for the handle, however, she pushed him away with such a shove he almost slipped off the float.

"Bugger off, I'm not a bloody imbecile," she yelled.

"Oi, what's the matter with you - you daft cow. He shouted back. "You almost had me in."

"Pity I didn't, sunshine. It might improve the smell around here."

Mercifully, she then flung open the cabin door and disappeared inside the plane, leaving a host of derelict expressions all glaring at me.

"You know, I think I'm starting to see why people have been taking pot shots at you," the Station Superintendent remarked, as he opened the door to the houseboat. "Shall we go inside? Hopefully it'll be a little bit quieter in there."

"I am so sorry about that," I continued. "It must be the heat or something. She doesn't usually behave like that."

"Don't worry, dear boy," he said, leading me into the empty saloon. "I once had a wife a bit like that."

He showed me to a seat by the window, before mixing himself a gin and tonic behind the bar. "Can I get you a drink?"

"No thank you very much," I replied.

"So is that shrew part of some noble experiment by your management?" he then enquired, as he sat down next to me. "Or do you have many women working on your 'boats?"

"I'm not sure exactly. I haven't been with the company very long," I replied. "Does Imperial Airways not employ any women then?"

"Certainly not as flight crew. Thank goodness. Although I've been told that an increasing number have been applying for positions as pilots, would you believe? Can you imagine that?" he laughed. "They'd probably be nipping off to the stern every five minutes to spend a penny or adjust their hair. Ridiculous idea. I'm sure that's a step too far even for you liberal minds at Imperial Air Services," he laughed.

"Quite possibly. Yes," I replied.

But, not for the first time, my sense of loyalty swelled just a little, like a lump in my throat; his scorn seemed to belong to a Dickensian world, which I was rather more used to hearing around the ring at the weekly mart.

"But there are some quite gifted female fliers around at the moment." I suggested, after a pause.

"Nonsense," he snapped back. "Half the time they seem to fall out the sky. Just look at that American girl: Amelia what's-her-name, disappeared without trace a couple of months ago. And the same goes for that old buzzard 'the Flying Duchess."

"You mean the Duchess of Bedford?"

"Yes, that's right."

"What happened to her - may I ask?"

"Took off in her Tiger Moth and was never seen again."

"I didn't hear about that. When did that happen?"

"Back in March or April, if I remember rightly. It was in all the newspapers."

"I must have been busy studying for my Finals," I muttered quietly, glancing out the window.

"Joy riders that's all. Serves them right in my book. They should leave flying to the professionals," he scoffed, before picking up a menu off the table. "Right, let's see what chef's cooking up this evening. Billy Cotton and his band are supposed to be coming in from Alexandria tonight on a world tour. I'm hoping they'll put on a bit of show and liven the place up a bit."

He went on to talk about some of other VIPs who had stopped with him during his tenure. But I found myself still gazing outside, watching as his mechanics doted upon our aircraft with a care and attention that almost warranted a sign saying Nil by Mouth. Fluids were fed in through umbilicals and it seemed that nothing was left to chance. However, as soon as the refuelling was done, Ms Hammond re-emerged from the aircraft and shouted something up at one of the mechanics on the wing. Another brief altercation ensued and my heart sank as they both clomped swiftly back toward the houseboat. Ms Hammond swept into dining room to address the passengers, while the mechanic stood before us in the saloon looking decidedly flustered.

"Excuse me sir," he said, a little unsure as to whom he should be addressing. "But I've just been informed by that stewardess - or whatever she is - that that aircraft is now leaving - although we're only about halfway through checking it over."

Both he and the Station Superintendent stared at me intently.

"Who exactly gives the orders on that old tub of yours?" the Superintendent finally enquired.

"Most of the time - it's the boss's daughter." I finally confessed.

"Oh I see. That clears that up," the Superintendent sighed solemnly, before turning to his mechanic. "Well there you have it, Alf. You've had your marching orders. Tell the boys to start packing everything away."

The mechanic immediately stormed out and all of Imperial Airways' methodical procedure was suddenly upended by Ms Hammond's ham-fisted demands. Mechanics struggled to get off the plane, while waiters bearing supplies began hurrying towards it. Behaving as graciously as I could, I bade farewell on behalf of the company, before joining the slow march of the passengers moving reluctantly along the pier. To a greater or lesser extent, we were all gripped by the same feeling of loss, as the embracing aroma of kippers and kedgeree gently loosened its grip.

23

Why exactly Ms Hammond was being so beastly toward our hosts was a complete mystery to me; nor could I understand why she was in such a rush to leave Basra. Nevertheless, I hurried into the cockpit, expecting to find her perched at the controls, desperate to get going. Instead, however, she was slumped on the floor with her head in her hands.

"Are you alright?" I asked, somewhat alarmed.

"Yes. Fine. Couldn't be better," she mumbled without looking up.

"Well, we're all set to go. Whenever you're ready."

"Good. Good," she said, showing little inclination to move.

"Would you like me to get us airborne?" I suggested, after a pause.

"No, no. I'll be fine. You just look after the passengers. I can hardly go out there looking like this!" she laughed.

She then lifted her hands from her face, revealing a severe bruise around her nose, which had rendered both eyes black and swollen.

"Are you sure you're OK to fly?" I enquired, as she began clambering to her feet.

"Yes, of course," she wheezed. "What a silly thing to say."

But as she tottered toward her seat, she stumbled and knocked a couple of rolled-up charts off the top of the navigator's desk.

"Goodness me I'm like an old lady today," she giggled, as I reached down and picked them up.

"By the way," I enquired hesitantly. "just in case any of the passenger's should ask - what's our next stop?"

"Karachi, of course," she answered, looking at me a little bewildered.

"Can we make it that far?"

"With a lean mixture and a tail wind, we'll get there," she said, shrugging her shoulders.

"But I was just speaking to the gentleman from *Imperial Airways* and he said that we wouldn't have sufficient range for Karachi."

"Oh, and he is the Captain of this vessel, is he?" she said, turning to face me with her head swaying a little.

"No, of course not," I replied.

"No. I am the Captain. And don't you forget it. Otherwise you'll be walking home," she snarled. "Do you understand?"

"I understand. But he did seem quite adamant."

"Excuse me?" she said, raising her voice. "Are you questioning my judgement?"

"No, of course not," I replied. "But - "

"But what?" she shouted, throwing her head back in disgust. "Christ. You know, I honestly thought that maybe, just maybe, you were a bit different from the rest of 'em. But you're all the bloody same, aren't you? Bunch of bloody washer women, that's all. All you want to do is sit around and have a good old gossip. Well, I tell you what," she spat, poking her finger into my chest. "why don't you bugger off into the kitchen - 'cos that's where you belong. Go on. Get out!" she screamed, pushing me out of the cockpit.

She slammed the door in my face, leaving my lame protest sitting like a gargoyle on my shoulder. Rightly or wrongly, I immediately wanted to apologise; perhaps my nerve had, finally, failed me. But I knew from experience that now she was in a place where only dumb animals and gelded beasts of burden were welcome; any further utterances from me were likely to be seen purely as an act of mutiny.

Besides, as soon as the engines fired up, it was a job simply staying on my feet. The aircraft lurched uncomfortably forwards and I had to brace myself in the doorway of the galley as we accelerated across the lake. I lost count of how many times we stalled and hit the water but I could hear the fuselage straining in $lb/inch^2$. It was the most bone-jarring take-off I have ever endured and by the time we got airborne the cupboards in the galley had puked most of our supplies onto the floor.

Tidying up the mess, however, seemed like fitting penance for my earlier lack of moral fibre. But, as we continued our faltering ascent, I kept gazing down at the floor as though it were some sort of oracle. My concerns were hardly alleviated when the door to the cockpit suddenly opened.

"Can I have a drink please?" Ms Hammond asked, blinking at me slowly.

"Of course," I replied, hurriedly reaching for the water jug, as the nose of the aircraft began to drop.

"No, no. I need something stronger than that. Give me a brandy. A large one," she insisted, before pulling a bottle of tablets out of her pocket.

She gripped it tightly in her hand, bleaching her knuckles white as I poured her out a stiff measure.

"Thank you," she said, carefully taking the glass before disappearing back inside the cockpit.

It was a relief seeing her looking more relaxed but leaving the controls whilst we were airborne was taking things a little far. Although the aircraft quickly regained its composure, I instinctively moved over to the window to check we were still on the right course. Sure enough, the coastline was leading us on as always and the view soon gave way to a reflection of frailties in the glass. So, once again, I turned my attention back to my duties as steward and the impending demands of the passengers.

Fortunately, thanks to *Imperial Airways'* catering, lunch required little in the way of preparation. I also assembled a sizeable spread for Ms Hammond, as I didn't want her to have any excuse to abandon the controls again. When I eased open the cockpit door with my offering, however, I still half-expected to be mauled by yet another piercing caterwaul. But she didn't react in any way as I placed it down beside her; she simply remained slouched at the controls, flying the aircraft with one hand while puffing on a cigarette with the other.

Without saying a word, I withdrew back to the galley and wondered if an equally warm reception was awaiting me in the passenger cabin. I peered through the curtain and saw the Blunderbuss wrapped in her manor house bumptiousness, while her disciples straddled the chilly narrows of the aisle. Almost all the men were fast asleep, seemingly struck down by the same weariness that was now undoubtedly affecting the crew. Ms Hammond's brother-in-law, however, was still wide awake; and, as I gazed at his amenable outlook, I suddenly remembered the offer he had made to don a dickie bow the night before.

Fortunately, he and Lady Ricardo were both sitting at the front of the cabin and I felt sure I could get his attention without alerting anyone else. But as I prized open a crack in the curtain, Ms Hammond once again emerged from the cockpit. Her hair was wet with perspiration and she seemed to take a long, measured breath before pushing me smartly to one side. She then dived headlong into the cabin and began belting out, what sounded like, Cole Porter's 'Anything Goes'.

I could feel the aircraft listing lazily to starboard but had to keep watching, completely agog like everyone else. She danced down the aisle ruffling fringes and tweaking cheeks until, finally, she twirled around at the stern - and promptly collapsed. Only her brother-in-law, H, responded with any decision; everyone else simply peered down at her in dismay and disgust. But he jumped out of his seat and raced to the back of the plane, while I staggered into the cockpit to bring the aircraft back onto an even keel.

When I eventually looked round over my shoulder, I thanked God that my responsibilities had compelled me to run away. Even from that distance I found myself suppressing the scream within us all. Ms Hammond was lying in a crumpled heap as if thrown from a dog's bite, while H administered procedures with a detached solemnity that I could never have matched.

But her face remained stubbornly stuck, seemingly only a shade or two away from oblivion. Every time he glanced up at the watching crowd H beseeched them, before politely despising their paltry tokens, such as hip flasks and smelling salts. Finally, he raised his head as if coming up for air and waded into the cockpit, kicking aside the remnants of Ms Hammond's lunch which was now lying strewn across the floor.

He lifted her jacket off the back of her seat and immediately began rifling through the pockets.

"Damn it!" he yelled as he pulled out a couple of empty pill bottles.

He made as if to hurl them onto the floor but refrained at the last moment and simply diminished to a crouch by my side.

"How long before we land?" he asked abruptly.

"I can't say for sure. Definitely a few hours to go," I replied.

"You couldn't put your foot down a little, could you? I'd prefer get to Karachi sooner rather than later."

"Well, we're already running at the limit of our range. But would you prefer it if I turned around?"

"No, no. Definitely not. There's a good hospital in Karachi. I know it quite well. And there's probably nowhere else within a thousand miles of here that has half-decent facilities."

"How are things back there?" I finally asked tentatively.

"Not great," he said biting his lip.

"What on Earth's happened to her?"

"I'm not sure - she seems to have overdone it."

"Is she going to be alright?"

"I don't know. Her pulse is very weak - and I really need to get some fluids into her as soon as possible."

"Well - help yourself to anything that's in the galley. There's some lunch back there as well."

"Do you want me to tell everyone else?"

"If you want - but I suppose you'd better explain it's a buffet."

"Sure. Sure," he nodded knowingly before retreating slowly from the cockpit.

It was almost as if some sort of contagion was degrading only the most robust on board. But now, at least, there was no longer any question as to whether we should still head for Karachi. I slackened off the mixture still further and began to pray for a tail wind, while H addressed the passengers briefly before kneeling down again next to Ms Hammond. He blanketed her with a silken shawl and started to remove her jewellery, which was like watching the flowers being taken from a hospital ward at the end of the day.

It did, however, go some way to soothe the bewilderment that had been clawing at the walls of the cabin. Eventually, the passengers started to funnel slowly into the galley before emerging meekly with their rations. They gazed at Ms Hammond but no one dared to suppose what was good for her anymore. Not that it mattered - because all the goodwill and taffeta in the world wasn't going to enhance the aircraft's endurance.

24

When I finally pieced together a more precise notion as to where we were on the map, I didn't have the courage to tell anyone at first. I simply clung to our itinerary as if it were some sort of religion - and began cajoling the plane like a horse. For a while, I even believed that, by straight-lining the coast, I might be able to glide toward Karachi and make a dead stick landing, slap bang in the middle of the harbour; or failing that simply let the currents take us in.

But when H again returned to the cockpit he laid his hand upon my shoulder, as if to say 'the game's up'.

"By the way, do you want anything to eat or drink?" he uttered. "Everyone's helping themselves but they seem to have forgotten about you."

"No thanks, I'm OK. How is she now?" I asked.

"No change - which can only be a good thing under the circumstances."

"Well, that's something," I said quietly, before slowly looking round. "We do have one other slight problem though."

"Oh what's that?"

"We're not going to make Karachi."

"What?" H replied in disbelief.

"We haven't got enough fuel. See for yourself," I said handing him the map. "I did try and warn Ms Hammond before we set off but she wouldn't listen to me."

"Was that what all that shouting was about earlier?"

"Yes, that's right."

"So what's the plan now then? Where are we going to land?"

"I really don't know. There doesn't seem to anything between here and Karachi except fishing villages."

"How close to Karachi do you think we can get?"

"I don't know - maybe within about 50 or 100 miles," I shrugged. "I can't say for sure. But I want to put down whilst there's still some daylight 'cos I've never landed this thing in the dark before."

"We need find somewhere pretty soon then," H said glancing at his watch. "Do you mind if I sit down and have a better look at this."

"Be my guest," I replied as he clambered into Ms Hammond's seat and opened out the map.

"Whereabouts are we now?"

"I think we crossed into India about an hour ago."

"Well, there's got to be some help we can call upon. In my experience, there's usually an office wallah sitting at a desk - even at the arse end of the Raj."

But his optimism petered out as we both peered into the distance. The aircraft simply went on skimming over miles of sandy shoreline, pockmarked by fishermen who were tending to their nets as if knitting fate. The only concession to progress was a larval sunset which left the instruments blushing and it became increasingly difficult not to lapse into a mournful hindsight.

There was no benevolence of Empire, as H had assured me - and I was already stiff from leaning hopefully forwards, when a crisp line of trees appeared. They shimmered in the breeze like the quickstep of a marching band and the aircraft immediately banked in the cross wind, as if urging me to take a closer look.

"What do you think that is?" I asked, turning toward H as we both strained to see over the side.

"I'm not sure. It's not a railway line is it? Looks remarkably straight and narrow," he replied.

"I was just thinking that. But there's no railway marked on the map - and I can't see any track."

But as we approached another small village, he suddenly jumped up and let out a yelp.

"Yes, look, it is a railway line!" he shouted, almost standing on the seat. "There's a water tower and a platform. And an engine shed," he beamed. "Now we can just land here and continue onto Karachi by train."

"But where do you suggest I land exactly?"

"Well this is a flying boat isn't it? Look, man, you're spoilt for choice."

"But how are we going to disembark? We need a harbour or a pier at the very least."

"For goodness sake. Just run it up the beach like those boys down there are doing. Shouldn't be too difficult. It looks nice and smooth. What's the draught on this thing? Can't be more than a few inches. At the very worst, I reckon, we'll get our shoes a bit wet."

He made it sound remarkably straightforward but beaching the aircraft certainly wasn't mentioned in any of the hypotheticals my instructor had given me. As I glanced at the fuel gauge, however, I could almost hear the engines busking on fumes, so I immediately swung the plane around and prepared the flaps.

"I suppose I'd better go and tell everyone the plan." H said getting up.

"No, no. Stay here," I said, grabbing his arm as I lined up for an approach.

He immediately sat down again and the aircraft dropped sharply as I cut the power. There was a sickening feeling of helplessness and I suddenly wished for so many things. I couldn't have had a more exemplary display of calm from my co-pilot, however; I simply wished it had been Ms Hammond because, as soon as we touched the water, I felt sure we would be remembering the moment one day at some distant party.

With gentle abandon, the aircraft glided serenely forwards and a dab on the throttles delivered us high and dry, squarely on the beach. The only evidence that our landing had been anything other than completely conventional was a slight list to starboard and a crack in the canopy glass.

"Nice one Skipper. Good job," H smiled with a wondrous look of nonchalance.

But it certainly wasn't shared by the gawping faces arrayed on the beach; or by any of the passengers, who were all looking feverishly out through the windows.

"Thanks - but I think I've got some explaining to do back there," I said looking round.

"Oh leave them to me. You go and make contact with the natives. Find out when the next train to Karachi leaves."

He muscled his way past me and immediately subdued the passengers with a loving patter that washed anyone's hands of any blame. But as I stepped out onto the float, the gravity of our situation suddenly pulled at all my qualifications. I found myself being watched by a crowd of men and boys amid a world of thatched huts and tent-flap amenities. When I pushed back my cap and waved, none of them responded; although, I suppose, I had no right to emerge from what amounted to a shipwreck with quite such a big grin. They simply went on looking at me fearfully and, as I approached, a young boy in a crisp, white shirt was hustled forwards like some bouquet - or sacrifice.

"Good afternoon. May I help you, sir?" he asked nervously, with his eyes and teeth gleaming almost as perfectly as his diction.

"Oh yes," I said somewhat taken aback. "I'm afraid we've run into a little trouble with our aeroplane. We were hoping to get a train from here to Karachi. Is that possible?"

"No, sir, not directly. The line is not yet completed, I am afraid. If you wish to get to Karachi, you have to take the line from here to Gorakh," he said with unerring expertise. "That line has been completed, sir. Then you change at Dadu and catch the mainline express."

"I see," I uttered slowly. "And about how long would that take? Can we get there tonight?"

"Oh no sir," he said gently shaking his head. "It will take many hours and you have already missed the connection with the express, I am afraid."

There seemed a certain inevitability as the hope in his eyes faded and, for once, it was no consolation when H stepped up to my side.

"But might I make a suggestion, sir?" the young boy went on, with his hands clasped together. "You could take the train from here to Gorakh. There is a small hill station there which you will be able to reach tonight."

"I didn't know there were any hill stations in this part of the world," H said, eyeing him and the rest of the crowd with some suspicion.

"It is newly built, sir. But it is very splendid. I have seen it for myself. There are some very comfortable lodgings. I am sure you will find it quite adequate. You could spend the night there and then go on to Karachi tomorrow."

"But how long will we have to wait for a train to get to this hill station?" H asked abruptly.

"Oh not long at all sir," the boy smiled. "You see, my father is the station master here and my friend's father, he is the engine driver. In the meantime, while you are waiting, my mother would be honoured to serve you and your guests some tea in the railway station."

He glanced around and pointed toward a clearing in the trees, where a paradigm of red-brick Victoriana was standing resolutely like a beacon.

"Well I don't suppose we can ask for better service than that," H said, with a sudden grin. "You don't know if there are any medical facilities at this hill station, do you?" he then asked the boy.

"That I do not know, sir. But there is a first aid post at the railway station. If that is some help."

"Let's go and have a look at it, shall we?" H said clapping hands and, together, they set off at a brisk pace up the beach.

Losing just one day from our schedule seemed like a fair trade, given the trauma we had suffered. But as I turned around it was obvious that our manifest was rather less enamoured by proceedings. They were already standing outside on the float, hanging onto the struts like flotsam; their faces were lashed by anguish and the sentiments that had flowered earlier in the cabin were now nowhere to be seen.

"Ladies and gentlemen," I called out. "Would you all like to follow me, there is some tea being served."

A couple of the men immediately jumped down onto the sand but the Blunderbuss and her gang didn't move.

"If you think you're fobbing us off with a cup of tea, young man, you're quite mistaken," she boomed with her familiar glare. "What on Earth are we doing here, stuck in the middle of nowhere? Are we going to Karachi now or not?"

"Not - exactly," I said delicately. "But I can assure you, we will be there first thing tomorrow."

"Tomorrow!" they all shrieked in unison.

"What about that poor stewardess?" the Blunderbuss went on. "She needs urgent medical attention."

"And what about our luggage?" Campari added looking toward the watching crowd. "We can't just leave it here unattended, that lot'll have it away in no time."

"Please, ladies and gentlemen," I insisted, counteracting them with my bare hands. "I will be bringing all the luggage with us on the train – which will be here very shortly to take us to our overnight accommodation. Then, as soon as I have resolved the problem with the fuel we will be continuing on from Karachi by air."

"Well, I'm not getting back in this tin can. It's an absolute liability," Campari cried, stepping sharply away from the plane.

"I quite agree," the Tweedy Gent's wife concurred, following her example. "This flight has been nothing but a disaster from beginning to end. As soon as we get to Karachi we're getting a boat," she wailed, turning to her husband.

"And I'm sticking with Imperial Airways - ," Lady Ricardo began, before being interrupted by a shout from H, who emerged from the tree line carrying a stretcher.

"Come on you lot, get moving. Tea's up," he said

ushering them all toward the railway station.

He seemed not to notice that most of the women were now close to tears. I had expected some operatics, of course; but not to that extent. With darkness descending and the tide coming in fast, however, there seemed no alternative except for everyone to persevere with H's cheery bombast.

The passengers trudged away up the beach, while I began emptying out the hold with help from some of the fishermen. H extracted Ms Hammond from the cabin and, as her limp body was stretchered past, I tried to look upon it as just another component that would soon be repaired. It didn't seem even remotely possible that anything more serious could go wrong. But long before I had finished removing all the bags, the momentum from what remained of our routines and procedures suddenly petered out.

A gaping hole appeared to swallow up every obscenity I could think of. Having been so sure of my landing, I gazed in disbelief at a ruptured section of the keel where all the rivets had been ripped out. There was no way that Ms Hammond's legend with all its accompanying miracles could fix this. But it wasn't until the luggage had been taken away that I found myself alone in the hold, gripped by self-loathing and hate.

I kicked the stoved-in fuselage more times than I care to remember before slamming the hatch door shut. I started across the sand, pulled by the stiff, sea breeze, but fell against the nearest tree.

"Please, sir. Come away from there," the young boy

immediately called out.

"Why? What's the matter?"

"It is very dangerous. If a coconut should fall, it could kill you."

"At the moment I couldn't care less," I replied, throwing my cap to the ground.

He remained beside me while I sat glaring at the clouds tapering across the sky and the sea foaming like champagne. All I hoped was that he wouldn't offer me any more hospitality because I truly feared some demonic outburst. I just wanted to get away from that pitiful little place where everything seemed to bend obligingly in the wind.

"Is your plane broken?" the boy finally enquired softly.

"Yes, you could say that," I muttered.

"I am sorry."

"It's hardly your fault."

"Well, I am sorry that the line to Karachi is not ready for you."

"Can't be helped," I shrugged.

"We hoped to have it finished but the other villages have not completed their sections of track. We are the only one to have done so, that is why the British governor rewarded us with the station - and the engine and both carriages. It is only a small engine, sir, but it is very strong and I know it will get you to Gorakh in no time. It came from Wales," he added cautiously after a pause. "Have you been to Wales, sir?"

"Once or twice - on holiday."

"I have heard it is a very beautiful place," he said, before edging a little closer. "But there is one thing I have always wanted to know, sir. The engine, it is called 'Og-wen', which is not a word I have come across in my studies. What does it mean exactly?"

"I don't believe it means anything. It's a Welsh name – a girl's name."

"Oh, my mother will be pleased," the boy smiled.

"Why's that?"

"Well, she has always wanted a daughter," he laughed, as a distant whistle blew. "Oh, that is her now, sir. Please, let me take you to her."

He helped me to my feet and we walked toward the station past retired dogs and old men stables, where women were nursing with breasts that were hanging exhausted.

"May I say, sir, it is wonderful to be speaking to a proper Englishman," the boy smiled, once again. "I have been studying English for some time now but I get very little chance to practice it."

"Well it's certainly paid off today." I smiled back.

"Oh thank you sir," the boy grinned. "I study using books my brother sends me. He is a lawyer in Delhi. One day, I hope to follow in his footsteps."

"Well, God knows, the world needs more lawyers," I replied.

As we came upon the station I didn't expect quite such a fanfare. But it seemed the whole village had turned out to hang garlands upon the little narrow-gauge loco - which looked like a hand-me-down from a slate quarry. The passengers, however, traipsed aboard cursing everything with spiked rhetoric, from the sand stuck on their shoes to the breeze tugging at their hats.

I gave them a wide berth and followed H into the end carriage. Ms Hammond was already lying on the floor with her limbs arranged loosely, as if her uniform was the only thing holding her together. When the train pulled away, I thanked the boy from the window and gave him the last pennies I had to my name. In return, he promised to take good care of the flying-boat, even though it had, doubtless, already been scuttled by the tide.

The train began snaking up toward the mountains, where there were few lights to adopt the night. Darkness and gloom clung to the sides of the carriage, which possessed just one Tilley lamp to fend them off. I sat staring at a promotion on the wall singing the praises of the Preseli Hills but H never looked up. He just gazed down at the floor and snapped instantly at any insect that landed upon Ms Hammond's body.

"Damn stupid girl," he mumbled to himself. "Shouldn't even be flying in her condition."

"What condition's that?" I asked.

"Consumption," he muttered through pursed lips. "Do you think you can find another pilot in the next day or so?"

"I don't know. But really it's another plane we need."

"Another plane?" he asked. "Why? What's wrong with

it?"

"I just had a look at the hull and it seems it didn't agree with our landing."

"Is it badly damaged? Surely it can be repaired?"

"Maybe," I shrugged. "I don't know."

"Oh Jeez," he said throwing his head into his hands and tearing at his scalp. "It's all my fault, isn't it?"

"No, no." I tried to reassure him. "If it wasn't for you we'd probably be floating around the Arabian Sea waiting to be rescued. Besides it's all pretty academic now 'cos I don't think we've any passengers left."

"Oh don't worry about them. They'll be alright by the morning," he scoffed. "And who knows, maybe this ol' cat will be up and running by tomorrow as well. She's a tough kid."

His smile was, by now, little more than a twitch but I still appreciated the blinkered bluster. As the train rattled on, however, Ms Hammond's unbuttoned blouse opened like a chrysalis; and I began to realise that to remain with her for anything less than forever was always likely to end in disappointment.

Eventually 'Ogwen' delivered us up to the hill station, where a timber-framed mansion was perched at the summit like an over-grown bird house. A retinue of knickerbockered manservants rapidly disembowelled the train and Ms Hammond was deposited in one of the many darkened bedrooms. The passengers, however, immediately assembled in the bar beneath standard lamps and the monocled gaze of stuffed fauna. They quickly began plotting like a coven, yearning to expose the extent of my idiocy - and to have Ms Hammond banished back to a land of sedated typing pools.

Their nightcaps became increasingly desperate measures that were downed in the flick of a wrist. As the drink dripped through their plastered minds, it stained their words brown. It wasn't until one of them tracked down a telephone, however, that I became more concerned; in those days, the right word in the right ear could affect the balance of the cosmos.

From almost anywhere in the building, I could hear them summoning up principles and rights as they sought to restore their blemished reputations. The commotion went on until the early hours and was even loud enough to wake Ms Hammond on a couple of occasions. But neither H nor myself could figure out what she said; we simply had to watch helplessly as guesses went begging all around her.

There was a mutual feeling of inadequacy between us, which persisted until another doctor suddenly appeared in the middle of the night. I don't know who had summoned him or where he had come from but he arrived with the one piece of equipment which I thought could make all the difference. Almost as soon as he had clambered out of his dusty old shooting brake, I stood poised to load Ms Hammond into the back. To my utter amazement, however, he was despatched empty-handed after a very curt discussion with H. He seemed determined not to let her go, citing the ungodly hour, amongst other things. As the car drove away, he simply went on religiously taking her pulse. I spent the entire night watching her residual pinkness battling the enveloping grey and had to wait until dawn before she could finally be moved.

Once again, the passengers scurried after their luggage, with one or two sparing a glance for Ms Hammond as we lifted her back into the train. We changed at Dadu, where our gilded skins got us a seat aboard a heaving express. It was here that I finally lost sight of the Blunderbuss and all the others; but myself and H still had to endure an asphyxiating journey with everyone around us gazing down at Ms Hammond as if she were the last of the trousered Amazons.

That day, perhaps, never really ended for her because, in the following weeks and months, all manner of entities emerged to scrutinise her story. Barristers, journalists and so-called experts all jockeyed to deliver a lexicon of disingenuous lather. I was quite sure, in my own mind, that success had never been available to her. But, unfortunately, it was they who would determine if that was fair and correct - or if Ms Hammond should be branded a failure.

Information regarding references and the publication of
'The Supermariner, Part 2' can be found at:

www.facebook.com/TheSupermariner